THE MIDNIGHT CHESS GAME

WOLFGANG ECKE

*Illustrated by Rolf Rettich
and Hansjörg Langenfass*

Translated from the German
by Stella and Vernon Humphries

Prentice-Hall, Inc.
Englewood Cliffs, N.J.

First American edition published 1985
by Prentice-Hall, Inc.
Englewood Cliffs, N.J.
First published in Great Britain 1985
by Methuen Children's Books Ltd
11 New Fetter Lane, London EC4P 4EE
Originally published in West Germany
by Otto Maier Verlag Ravensburg
in volumes entitled:
Das Schloss der roten Affen, Der Mann in Schwarz,
Das Geheimnis der alten Dschunke, Das Gesicht an der
Scheibe, Solo für Melodica, Das Haus der 99 Geister,
Schach bei Vollmund and *Keine Spur von Paul Crabbley*

Library of Congress Cataloging in Publication Data

Ecke, Wolfgang, 1927–1983
    The midnight chess game

    Summary: A collection of mysteries for the reader to solve,
with explanations and solutions in the back of the book.
    1. Detective and mystery stories, German—Translations
into English.   2. Detective and mystery stories, English—
Translations from German.   3. Children's stories, Ger-
man—Translations into English.   4. Children's stories,
English—Translations into German.   [1. Mystery and
detective stories.   2. Short stories.]   I. Rettich, Rolf, ill.
II. Langenfass, Hansjörg, ill.   III. Title.
PZ7.E1975Mi   1985   [Fic]   84-26564
ISBN 0-13-582826-0

CONTENTS

   * easy
  ** quite difficult
*** difficult

THE MIDNIGHT CHESS GAME

The moon was full that summer night. Every now and then, thick banks of cloud piled into dense masses, only to float away again, leaving no trace. The effect was disturbing, exciting even, as brilliant moonlight gave way to inky darkness, only to return, more dazzling than ever. It was a night for witches and goblins—and for burglars.

The lights had just gone out all over Richard Morgan's large house in a smart Berlin suburb called Dahlem. Morgan was a rich man, the owner of an important shoe factory. But tonight he tossed and turned in his bed, as he always did when the moon was full. For a long time he had tried to get to sleep by solving a chess problem in his head. But it was the fiendishly difficult one laid out on the table beside his bed, and it had had quite the opposite effect. It was past two o'clock, and he was more wide awake than ever.

Twelve midnight

Slowly, slyly, the moon re-emerged from behind a wall of cloud. Morgan watched the burst of silver light come flooding through the half-open balcony door of his second-floor bedroom.

Suddenly he started. Was it really happening, or was he dreaming? Someone seemed to be pushing silently at the balcony door. A dark figure in jeans came into view. Over the man's head was a hood, and over the hood was a half-mask with eye-slits. The stranger wore gloves.

Morgan kept perfectly still. Then the intruder caught sight of him. His hand flashed inside his shirt and whipped out a pistol. He tiptoed to the bed, while Morgan held his breath, watching the newcomer's every movement.

All at once, the intruder paused, fascinated by the state of play between the small ivory chesspieces on the table.

"Aha! A fellow chess player, I see," remarked Morgan softly. The man was startled and pointed his pistol straight at Morgan's head.

"So you're awake after all," he hissed. "Don't do anything silly, or. . . ."

"Put that idiotic thing down before you do

some damage," said Morgan calmly. "I'm not armed."

"You never can tell," muttered the stranger, his eyes returning to the chessboard. "Good for white, though," he went on. "Mate in three!"

"Impossible!" Morgan contradicted him. "I've been awake half the night trying to solve it, and it can't be done."

The burglar transferred the pistol from his right to his left hand. "Look!" he said, gloating a little. "If the white knight checks like this, the black king is forced into one of two options. But with the bishops covering the other squares, mate in three it is!"

"You're absolutely right!" Morgan shook his head in admiration. "Nice work! You're the man I've been waiting for."

"You're pulling my leg," said the intruder. "How could you know I'd come?"

"Whenever I can't sleep, I keep hoping some-one will drop in for a game, and especially when there's a full moon. And here you are!"

"Who else is there in the house?" asked the man suspiciously.

"There's only my wife—her room is down the hall, but she'll be fast asleep—and the house-keepers who sleep in the room below this one. No one else. But by the way," asked Morgan in-nocently, "what exactly do you want?"

"What do I want?" echoed the stranger mockingly. "Just to relieve you of any spare cash you have lying about. Got it?"

"I see. You've come to rob me. In that case, Tom. . . ."

"I'm not Tom. My name's Felix. What's yours?"

"I'm Richard Morgan. I have a factory that makes shoes. But listen to me, Felix. Let's have a gentleman's agreement. We'll play one game of chess—chess by moonlight. If you win, I'll hand over my wallet and my gold watch."

"But suppose I lose?" Felix scratched his head with the barrel of his gun.

"Then you'll go away empty-handed. And if you keep your side of the bargain, I give you my word, I won't call the police. That's fair, isn't it?"

Felix looked at the chess game, then back at Morgan. "Okay, it's a deal. But let's move the table nearer to the balcony. The light's better over there."

With a sigh, Richard Morgan heaved himself out of bed. "As you please."

The moon was so bright that every detail stood out clearly. After several moves, Morgan leaned back, mightily satisfied with himself. His opponent was crouching over the table, sulking. "You and your pawns," he muttered, "they're driving me nuts."

Richard chuckled. "They're my specialty. I'm all for pawn attack and pawn play generally. Check!"

"Check? Where?"

"Here . . . with the rook."

"This idea of yours is crazy," growled Felix. "I should never have agreed."

"Nonsense, you could still win. One mistake on my part and. . . ."

But Morgan never finished the sentence. At that moment, the bedroom door was flung open and the ceiling light was switched on. Dazzled for a few seconds, both men turned. Two women in bathrobes were standing in the doorway. The older woman, who was the Morgans' housekeeper, gave a shriek. "There! I told you so!"

The younger one turned to her husband. "What on earth are you doing, Richard? Mrs. Crumb thought she saw a man climbing past her window and over your balcony. And as Mr. Crumb refused to believe her and went back to sleep again, she came to wake me."

"Felix and I are playing chess. Felix is a burglar, and if he wins, he gets my wallet and my watch."

Felix had grown impatient. He sprang to his feet and snatched up his pistol.

"B–b–but he's armed!" stammered Helena Morgan, while Mrs. Crumb clutched the door-post, white as a sheet.

"Don't call for help or I'll shoot!" said Felix. "But first of all, hand over that watch and your wallet!"

Morgan obeyed meekly. He was taking no risks. Quick as a flash, Felix pocketed both objects.

"I protest," said Richard. "The game isn't over. You remember our gentleman's agreement, don't you?"

"Forget it, boss . . . I'm off!"

In less time than you would have believed possible, Felix had dashed to the balcony, climbed over the railing and landed on the ground, a ten-foot drop. By the time Morgan had run after him, there was no sign of Felix.

Mike's Bar and Grill was still quite full, although it was past two o'clock in the afternoon. The customers were a mixed bag of hungry and thirsty passersby, but among them were several small-time crooks, who believed they were safe for the moment. They knew that the police liked to keep an eye on the place, just in case.

Felix the chess player was sitting at the back of the room, a bowl of soup in front of him. At first, he didn't notice a thin little man eyeing him from the door. It was only when the man was standing beside him that Felix looked up.

"Well, I'll be a monkey's uncle! If it isn't Eddie!"

He was delighted to see his friend. "I thought you were in the clink for another three months!"

"They knocked off a bit for good behavior," said Eddie.

"That's great! When did you get out?"

"The day before yesterday," replied Eddie, staring at Felix's glass of beer with undisguised envy.

"Had a crack at anything yet?" asked Felix.

"No, it's too soon. I've got to go into training first. Nothing's worse for a pickpocket than being out of practice," grumbled Eddie, cracking his joints and spreading out his spidery fingers like a Siamese temple dancer.

"Ugh! Stop it!" shuddered Felix. "You're ruining my appetite."

"Buy me a beer," whined Eddie. "I'm broke."

Felix did not need to be asked twice. "Vera!" he called. "A glass of beer for Eddie here, and a double Scotch for me!"

"Whiskey, eh? You must be in the money!"

Felix nodded. "Last night," he explained, trying not to boast, but not quite succeeding, "I cleaned out a shoe manufacturer. See this? It's crammed full."

"Some wallet!" said Eddie admiringly, laying it on thick. "Real crocodile leather. I bet it holds a bundle."

Felix then showed him the expensive gold watch. Eddie whistled, deeply impressed.

"One double, one beer," said the waitress putting down the glasses.

"Thanks," said Felix, paying for the drinks.

"Thanks," said Eddie. His mind was racing. "Say, Felix, old buddy, I don't suppose you'd help out a pal with a few bucks, would you? You're in the money, after all, and you know what it's like when you come out of the clink."

"It's a pleasure," said Felix grandly. He had his faults, but he was never stingy. He handed Eddie a crackling new fifty dollar bill from Morgan's wallet. "Let's call it my good deed for the day," he said with a flourish, and returned to his bowl of soup, which was getting cold.

"Boy, oh boy!" exclaimed Eddie, out of the blue. "Is that clock right?"

"Sure. Just two-thirty. Why? What's the hurry?"

"I've got to get going. I promised to pick up my sister. I'd forgotten all about it!" Eddie got up so quickly that his raincoat must have caught on the chair, for as he rose, he stumbled on top of Felix and the soup splashed all over the place, most of it in Felix's face.

"Take it easy!" he cried indignantly. "Gee, what a mess!"

"Sorry, pal," Eddie said. "I'll ask someone to come and clean it up. I must have got my foot caught somehow." He slapped his friend on the shoulder, while Felix wiped the soup from his left eye and his right cheek. "See you around, Felix! Good luck!" And Eddie was gone.

Felix followed Eddie with his eyes. His brain was not working as fast as usual. . . . Gone to pick up his sister, was he? Since when did Eddie Miller have a sister? He'd always said he had no family—claimed he was brought up in an orphanage. Glancing down at the table, Felix noticed Eddie's untouched glass of beer. He hadn't even tasted it, something he'd never done before in all his life.

In a flash, the truth dawned. Dry-mouthed, Felix groped for Morgan's wallet. It had vanished . . . and the gold watch with it.

Out of practice, was that what Eddie had said? He'd have to go into training?

Felix was furious, partly at his sheer helplessness, but most of all because he had been let down. He'd always thought of Eddie as a real pal.

"Good afternoon, Felix!"

Felix looked up. "This is a surprise, Inspector."

"Not for me," replied Inspector Humbert dryly. "I've been looking for you."

"Me?" Felix's face was the picture of innocence. "What for?"

"The Dahlem job last night."

"I don't know what you're talking about, honest."

"You weren't up to your usual tricks in Dahlem last night?" the inspector insisted.

"Never! Not me! Who was burgled?"

"A man named Morgan. Owns a shoe factory. He says the thief told him his name was Felix. Not a very common name, is it?" grinned Humbert.

"No, that's true, but anyone caught in the act could give another fellow's name, it's as easy as pie. Besides," Felix added with dignity, "I'd never rob a fellow chess player!"

"So you're saying someone did it to frame you? Is that your story?"

"It is," said Felix firmly. "By the way, what was taken?"

"A wallet stuffed with hundred dollar bills, and a valuable gold watch." Felix whistled through his teeth. Then an idea struck him. "Why don't you search me, Inspector? If you find any of the stolen loot on me, you can arrest me here and now."

"Even if your pockets are empty, Felix, I'm still going to run you in. You've just given yourself away, as good as confessed everything. . . ."

"Me?" Felix looked bewildered. "But I haven't admitted a thing!"

"Oh yes, you have. You said one sentence too many. All the same, here's a piece of news that may cheer you up. We've just collared Eddie Miller. He's a bit out of practice, poor devil . . .

caught him in the act, trying to snatch a lady's handbag. And he had Morgan's watch and wallet on him, the ones he swiped from you. Of course he tried to make out it was all your fault, you know what a rat he is. . . ."

What was the "sentence too many" that caught Inspector Humbert's attention? How did Felix the burglar give himself away?

THE FLAT TIRE

On a May night between Thursday and Friday, a person or persons unknown broke into the branch of the American Bank in Assisi, Italy, probably just after midnight. They cared nothing for the fact that Assisi was the birthplace of Italy's gentlest saint, Saint Francis. Having disconnected the alarm system, the thieves used acetylene torches to cut into the vault. They left no other clues. They got away with 500 million lire.

Mario Morti was shaving when he heard the 5 A.M. news on the radio. Morti owned a small gas station and garage not far from the town of Spoleto. He liked to make an early start. His wife Anna and the three-year-old twins, Aldo and Gina, were still asleep in the apartment above the garage when he tiptoed down the stairs.

As he opened the double doors of the garage, he saw an unusual sight. A well-dressed man was coming down the road, bent double as he tried to roll a car wheel with a completely blown-out tire. By the time he reached the garage, he was soaked with sweat. He straightened up and, holding his back, he groaned and spluttered, "I couldn't have gone another step! Do you have a spare tire like this in stock?"

Mario glanced at it. "No, I don't have a spare but I can fix that one for you. Where did it happen?"

The customer pointed down the road. "About a mile from here. It was still quite dark and today of all days, I didn't have a spare in the trunk."

Mario Morti was a friendly soul and he started chatting as he worked. "Heard the news on the radio?" he asked.

"No, I don't have one in my car. Anything special?"

"I'll say! A robbery at the American Bank!"

The customer didn't seem interested. "Do you call that news? Why, there's one every week almost. Serves the Americans right."

"Things are going to the dogs," sighed Mario. "It won't be safe to go out soon."

"Oh, it's not as bad as the papers make out. They always lay it on thick."

"It's bad enough!" retorted Mario.

"How much did the crooks get away with?" asked the customer.

"Five hundred million, so they said," Morti informed him.

"Phew!" whistled the man. "It's hard to believe."

"How do you mean?"

"That a bank in a quiet little place like Assisi would have so much cash in the vaults. I'll bet it's another exaggeration."

"Perhaps it was a special consignment and the thieves were tipped off."

"Could be." The man didn't seem too interested. Then he asked "Will I be able to get to Rome by ten?"

"Are you in such a hurry?"

"Yes, I have to catch a plane."

"Lucky you, going by plane. I can't afford it." Mario was bending over the tire, so the other man did not see the strange gleam in his eye.

The customer repeated his question impatiently. "I must be in Rome by ten o'clock, or rather at the airport. Can I do it?"

"I should think so, in a fancy Lancia sports car like yours. I expect you really step on the gas."

"You better believe it."

"You don't need to worry, then. As soon as the tire's ready, I'll drive you back to your car."

Fifteen minutes later, Mario's Fiat had drawn up beside the jacked-up Lancia Beta. In another five minutes, the wheel was back in place and the car could be driven away. The customer was grateful and gave Mario a lavish tip. Again he failed to notice the look in Morti's eyes, so he could not guess that the moment Mario arrived back in his garage, he went straight to the phone.

Inspector Luigi Ovalli frowned. "Who's speaking?" he barked.

"Mario Morti from the garage outside Spoleto. I believe I've recognized one of the Assisi bank robbers."

Ovalli was all attention. "Can you repeat that? We have a terrible connection."

Mario did as he was asked and added, "He walked into my repair shop with a flat tire."

"What was he driving?"

"A dark green Lancia Beta, license number Rome 2299145. He's on his way to the airport. I thought I should report it."

At 9:46 A.M., a dark green Lancia Beta was stopped six miles north of Rome. In the car, the police found bank notes to the value of 500 million lire.

The question for you is this: What aroused Signor Mario Morti's suspicions? How did he guess that this early morning customer had something to do with the bank robbery?

THE JOYRIDE

The sky in Stockholm that June morning was palest blue. The clock had just struck five. Professor Berg rose from his desk, stretched himself and switched off the light. Once again he had worked through the night. He drew back the curtains from both windows and looked down on the empty street.

Then he started back in dismay, his eyes staring. The smart Volvo sports car he had bought only last Thursday was no longer where he had left it the evening before.

The professor rushed to the phone.

5:30 A.M.
The police at last! Professor Berg had been dozing off, as he waited. "I'm Inspector Orndal," said

the officer on the doorstep. "Sorry to have kept you waiting, but we're shortstaffed. Can you describe the car concerned?"

"It's a Volvo sports car, and it's brand new!"

The inspector looked at Berg with raised eyebrows. "A white Volvo 1800 with red leather seats, and a license number ending in 66?"

"That's it!" exclaimed Berg, not concealing his surprise. "But how could you possibly know that? I didn't give any details over the phone."

"It's standing by the curb," answered Orndal, pointing.

The professor could hardly believe his eyes. "Yes, that's it!" he agreed. Then, pursing his lips, he added, "It must have been one of the Sixten twins who took it for a joyride. They're completely out of control."

"Please explain," said the inspector tersely.

"They lost their parents a few years ago, and they live alone in that big house opposite. Carsten has the rooms upstairs, while Leo lives on the ground floor. They're two young rowdies, and when they're not quarreling, they're always into mischief. There's hardly any trouble in this neighborhood that doesn't involve one or both of them."

"How old would they be, these Sixten twins?"

"Twenty-three or twenty-four, I imagine," answered the professor.

"I think I'll go and see what they're up to," replied the inspector. "Good morning, Professor. I'll call you if I've any news."

The big isolated house, the home of the terrible twins, showed no sign of life. All the shutters except for one on the ground floor were shut tight. Orndal walked round the outside and then approached the front door. He was still some distance from it when it flew open and a young man in a canary yellow bathrobe stood in the doorway. He was pointing an old-fashioned shotgun.

"Don't move," he shouted. "Stay where you are!"

The police officer ignored the order. "That's pretty ancient, isn't it?" he said, referring to the gun. "Must have been hanging on a wall, right?"

"Mind your own business! We don't like prowlers here!"

"I'm Detective Inspector Orndal," he announced. "Are you Leo or Carsten Sixten?"

"Leo. What do you want anyway?"

"I'm here because Professor Berg across the street believes you took his car for a joyride this morning."

"You must be joking!" retorted the young man. "I'm not guilty, I assure you. In fact, I came home less than five minutes ago."

"I suppose you'd been for a nice walk," said Orndal sarcastically.

Leo Sixten flicked away a half-smoked cigarette. "Right! You're not as dumb as most cops, I must admit. That's just what I did. I went for a nice long walk."

"Where exactly?"

"Here and there, up and down, you know. I've been on my feet for a good three hours. Walking is a hobby of mine." Here Leo paused and put his head on one side. "I've got an idea, Inspector. Why not talk to my brother Carsten upstairs? I wouldn't put it past him to do such a thing. He's car crazy, you know. Besides, he only came home shortly after five."

Inspector Orndal eyed the young man. "I think I'll do just that," he chortled, as if something had amused him very much.

Carsten Sixten was in his pajamas when he opened the door of his studio apartment to Inspector Orndal's knock. He mumbled something not very polite and pointed to a chair. As the inspector sat down, Carsten crawled back into bed. He said nothing at all.

At last the inspector spoke. "At least you don't seem to be surprised to see the police in the house at this hour of the day. Don't you want to know why I'm here?"

"I am sure you'll explain," said Carsten, yawning. "Frankly, I couldn't care less."

"I will indeed explain. Your brother thinks you borrowed Professor Berg's new car for a joyride early this morning."

Carsten sat up with a jerk. "Leo's always telling whoppers," he sneered. "I'm not interested in the professor's car, nor what he has for lunch, nor the color of his nightshirt! Looking after Number One is enough for me!" Then he added, "Besides, I've got a car of my own." Having made his statement, he slumped back and yawned again.

"What time did you come home this morning?"

"I didn't look at the clock," the youth answered. "It must have been about ten past five, though."

"Have you any witnesses?"

"No. I don't know if Leo was home yet."

Inspector Orndal got to his feet. "May I use your phone?" he asked. His face gave nothing away.

"Do what you like. It's in the hall outside. Now can I go back to sleep? I can hardly keep my eyes open."

"I'm not stopping you."

Inspector Orndal left the bedroom, found the telephone and dialed Professor Berg's number.

When Berg answered, the inspector spoke loudly enough to be heard downstairs as well as upstairs.

"This is Inspector Orndal speaking, Professor. I wanted to tell you that you were quite right. One of the Sixten brothers was responsible for taking your car. Yes, you can go ahead if you wish to prosecute."

As the inspector left the house, one twin was furious, but completely at a loss. He had no idea what to do next.

Which of the Sixten brothers is the chief suspect, Leo or Carsten?

AT DEAD
OF NIGHT

Jason Fry had been on Interpol's *Wanted* list for almost two years. He was the head of an international ring, expert forgers of credit cards. Yet in spite of the efforts of the police of many countries, Fry remained at liberty. He must have been able to disguise his appearance at will, and also to move from country to country without being spotted.

One fine September morning, an anonymous letter landed on the desk of Detective Inspector Riley in Dublin, Ireland. With growing amazement, the officer read the following:

> *If I'm not mistaken, you have been looking for Jason Fry, the credit card forger, for the last couple of years. You may like to know that he is living under the assumed name of*

Dr. Oscar Grey in Finnegan Square. I hope
you catch him and I shall call for my reward
once he is under lock and key.

A well-wisher

Inspector Riley easily confirmed that there
was a Dr. Oscar Grey living at 13 Finnegan
Square, but he was more puzzled than ever to
see that the man called himself an ornithologist.
An ornithologist is an expert on birds and Inspector Riley could not for the life of him see
any connection between forged credit cards and
bird studies. All the same, he started further inquiries, and in half an hour, he had learned that
Dr. Grey had rented the house only eighteen
months before. Nothing was known against him.

Was it a genuine tip-off, or was someone simply trying to make mischief?

Riley had the house in question watched for
two days and two nights, but without result. If
there was anything fishy going on, it could not
be detected from the outside.

Late on the evening of the third day, Riley
decided he would go there himself, accompanied
by Sergeant Murphy. They would not be in uniform. "I wonder if all fraud merchants live in
such plush surroundings," mused the sergeant
as they arrived in front of the house. A clock was
chiming midnight.

"Only the most successful ones," replied Riley. He pointed to the blaze of lights shining from the windows. "I wouldn't like his electricity bill for a start," he added grimly.

Detective Inspector Riley had no plan of action, but he knew he must tread warily. After all, apart from the anonymous letter, he had nothing whatever to go on.

The slim gentleman of medium height who answered their ring must have been about forty years old. He wore a green silk bathrobe with the initials OG embroidered on the pocket. He had black hair and his dark eyes flashed at the sight of his unexpected visitors. The strangest thing about him, however, was the pair of birds on his shoulders. On the left was a sleek raven, and on the right perched a rook which had had its wings clipped.

"Dr. Grey?" asked Riley politely.

The birdman was equally polite, although the raven stabbed at Sergeant Murphy with its beak. "Yes, that's right. What can I do for you?"

"I'm Detective Inspector Riley and this is my colleague, Detective Sergeant Murphy. We'd like a word with you, if it's not too much trouble."

Dr. Grey seemed surprised but he waved a hand, inviting them indoors. "Please come in, gentlemen. Visitors who arrive at dead of night

are always the most interesting," he added sarcastically in a strong foreign accent. The two birds screeched and squawked, but Grey shooed them into a small room off the hall. Then he showed the visitors into his study.

There were birds everywhere. Some were stuffed but others were very much alive. In all there were fourteen cages of varying sizes and as if at a word of command, their occupants began twittering and chirping. As Dr. Grey ushered the officers toward two easy chairs, he covered the cages with blue cloths. Before long, there was complete silence in the large room.

"Now then, gentlemen, how can I help you? I take it you haven't called to discuss birds. Or have you?"

"You're right about that," smiled Riley. "I don't have to tell you, Dr. Grey, that a policeman's duty can sometimes be unpleasant. . . ." Here he paused to observe the man opposite. But apart from his courteous attention, Grey showed no reaction whatsoever, and waited patiently for Riley to go on.

"The other day, we received an anonymous letter, informing us that you are really Jason Fry, a very much wanted person," he continued, "and wanted in more than one country."

Dr. Grey opened his eyes wide and shook his head as if completely mystified.

"Does Fry's name mean anything to you, Dr. Grey? Or do you know who might have written us such a letter?" asked Riley.

"You've put it very tactfully, but I'm afraid I must disappoint you, Inspector. I've never heard

of this Jason Fry and as for an anonymous letter
. . . I have no idea who wrote it." He seemed
more puzzled than alarmed at what he had heard.

"May we see your passport?"

"With pleasure," said Grey. He went to his
desk, took a passport from a drawer and handed
it to the inspector, who passed it over to Murphy.
The sergeant was an expert on forged passports.

Murphy examined the document carefully. "All
in good order," he said finally before handing it
back to its owner. As Grey replaced it in the
same drawer, he forced a smile as if remember-
ing something from the past. "Come to think of
it, I was once mistaken for the director of a Swiss
zoo, but I've never been confused with a credit
card forger before. To be frank, the previous
mix-up was less offensive. All the same, may I
offer you a drink?"

The two officers had already risen. "No, thank
you, Dr. Grey," said Riley. "Late as it is, we still
have work to do." They apologized once more
for their intrusion and said goodbye.

When they were in the street again, Murphy
said angrily, "Confound these anonymous letters!
It was damned awkward, wasn't it, Chief?"

The inspector disagreed. "I wish they were all
so helpful. For once, this one told the truth. Go
and get a warrant for the arrest of Grey *alias* Fry.
And make it snappy. I'll stay around and make

sure this most valuable bird of ours doesn't fly away."

"B–b–but the p–p–passport was genuine, I'd swear to that!"

"The passport perhaps. But on your way to headquarters, think about what was said. You'll soon realize the slip our birdman made."

What was the slip Riley referred to? In other words, how did the false Dr. Grey give himself away?

THE ROLAND SQUARE MYSTERY

It was nearly 5:30 P.M. one dreary February evening in London. Benjamin Benford was about to close up his camera and computer shop in Roland Square for the day, when two customers showed up. Before Mr. Benford could ask them what they wanted, they put on masks, sprayed something into the air and he lost consciousness. When he came to, the men had simply disappeared, taking with them cameras, videocassette recorders, and microcomputers worth several thousand pounds in all.

The next day, Mr. Benford was invited to police headquarters at Scotland Yard Street to study the vast collection of photographs in the Rogues' Gallery. He could identify one of the burglars as a well-known criminal, Stan Boston. Unfortunately, however, the Robbery Squad couldn't trace Boston's present address, in spite of all their efforts.

The next best thing was to look for a former accomplice of Boston's, Tom Webster. Here they had more luck. He ran straight into their arms in a notorious Soho neighborhood hideout. But then their luck ran out. Once in custody, Webster stoutly denied any part in the Roland Square raid; and as the police had no evidence against him except his old association with Boston, it looked as if they would have to let Webster go.

Constable Leslie Hill was the "new boy," the most recent recruit to the Police Robbery Squad. He looked even younger than he was. With his solemn face and gold-rimmed glasses, you might have mistaken him for a lanky schoolboy. The three experienced officers with whom he worked liked Les, but privately they thought he wasn't tough enough. His soft, almost lilting voice didn't fit in with the Scotland Yard image.

Constable Hill was well aware of his colleagues' misgivings, but he was both intelligent and patient. He knew he had to win his spurs and he spent his time learning how to examine so-called witnesses and to perform other routine tasks. Even when he was teased, Les remained even tempered. He never whined or refused a job, however humdrum. He remained friendly and cooperative—a good pal to all—and accepted the fact that he had still to earn the others' respect.

When Tom Webster was "run in," Hill's senior colleagues set to work on him. First Detective Inspector Calloway interrogated the suspect, then Detective Sergeants Morgan and Newton took turns trying to get the truth out of him.

Webster kept his head. He protested his innocence. He couldn't have had anything to do with the Roland Square affair, because he hadn't seen Stan Boston for a good five years, not since they had shared an apartment in the city of Sheffield, in fact. He had lost touch with Stan completely, and had no idea where he was living in London.

Since Mr. Benford, the shopkeeper who had been robbed, had failed to identify the second man in the case, things began to look bad for the police, but pretty good for Tom Webster.

Inspector Calloway leaned back in his chair, exhausted. "If we can't find some evidence against Webster within the next hour or two, we'll have to let him go!"

It was then that Constable Hill dropped his bombshell. He asked a favor in his slow, quiet voice. "May I have a word alone with the suspect, Inspector? I've an idea of my own, and I think it may work."

The three experienced officers looked at Hill as if he'd gone out of his mind. He in turn knew what they were thinking: If *we* can't get anything out of Webster, how can this babe-in-arms succeed? But it didn't worry the young man, not in the least.

Inspector Calloway tried not to smile, but as he couldn't think of any good reason for refusing, he consented. "Why not, Les? You have a try by all means while we take a break. But I warn you, Tom Webster is a tough nut to crack!"

Tom Webster eyed Constable Hill with a mixture of suspicion and amusement. "Hello," said Hill. "Cigarette?" He offered the packet to the man in custody and sat down opposite him.

Webster didn't want to smoke. He seemed to be sizing up the young officer. "Hey!" he sneered. "You look more like a kid out of nursery school than a graduate of the Police Academy! If you ask me, the Yard's been robbing the cradle!"

"It's not so long since I left school, I admit," nodded Les, "but here I am at Scotland Yard. I can hardly believe it myself."

"Things have come to a pretty pass, I must say. But I'll wear you all down before I let you arrest me again," declared Tom defiantly.

"You nearly had us beat," Les Hill conceded, "but I'll give you credit for one thing. Calloway & Co. have never had to work so hard to make a hoodlum crack before. Congratulations!"

Webster frowned. He didn't know what to

make of this line of talk and he fidgeted restlessly on the edge of his chair. "What's all this baloney?" he blurted out at last. "Is it a new trick to try and trip me up? I had nothing to do with that break-in, I've already told your pals that over and over again."

"You don't have to bluff it out for me," Leslie Hill assured him. "I'm only here to take notes. I'm too wet behind the ears for a serious case like this. Mind you, I caught a pickpocket in the act the other day."

Tom Webster was baffled. What had pickpockets to do with him, a master criminal? Why on earth had the inspector sent him this half-wit?

Hill carried on unperturbed. "Not bad for a beginner, don't you agree?"

And when Webster did not bother to reply, Les pretended to be offended. "Oh, I know I'm not ready to catch a big fish like you, I'm just a rookie."

Tom's self-control was on a knife-edge with sheer exasperation. "If I met you alone on a dark night, I'd make mincemeat of you!" he spluttered.

"Then you'd be out of luck, mate," smiled Les. "I'm a Black Belt!"

"I couldn't care less," snapped Tom. "You bore me. Tell your boss I had nothing to do with the Roland Square job and that I want to go home."

"Sorry, Webster, perhaps I shouldn't tell you

· **40** ·

this, but it's all sewn up. You've had it!" Here Les Hill lowered his voice so that Webster had to bend forward to hear him. "You insisted that you hadn't been in touch with Stan Boston since you were in Sheffield together five years ago. Is that still your story?"

"So it's finally sunk in, has it?" jeered Webster. "You've got it right!"

"And you haven't seen Boston again since you came back to London?"

"Right again!"

"It isn't, you know," said Hill quietly. "Boston squealed on you this morning. He says that you and a man from Dover raided the shop in Roland Square."

Webster's veins stood out on his forehead as he clenched and unclenched his fists. "He's a liar," he croaked, his eyes rolling.

"He's prepared to swear it," the constable went on. "We had to let Boston go. His alibi was water-tight. Oh, I've just remembered—he said you and Joe Bradley were the ones. He's ready to go on the witness stand."

"The dirty dog!" shouted Tom Webster. "It's all lies. He wants me to carry the can."

"I'll make you a suggestion, Webster. Why don't you phone Boston yourself and tell him what you think of him?" And Hill pushed the phone over to Tom.

The latter did not need to be asked twice. He pounced on the phone and his fingers were trembling as he dialed the seven digits of Boston's number.

"Busy!" he mumbled and then dialed again. "Still busy!" He paused for a moment and then tried a third time. "Still busy . . . same again." He tried twice more and then gave up. It was no good. Furiously he gave the phone a shove and it went crashing to the floor. Tom did not guess that on this extension phone, you always got the busy signal unless you dialed a special code first. He sat slumped on his chair, snorting and muttering in turn. "Why . . . why . . . why has Boston pulled this dirty trick on me?"

Constable Leslie Hill got up, hastily scribbling something on a pad. He made for the door and left Webster alone with his thoughts.

Detective Inspector Calloway and his colleagues, Morgan and Newton, looked up as Hill rejoined them.

"What made Webster blow his top? Did you stick pins in him?" asked Newton.

"And what was that crash?" Morgan wanted to know.

"It was only the phone. Webster pushed it off the table."

"Why would he do that?"

"He was peeved because he couldn't get through to Stan Boston. The number was busy. Here it is, incidentally. Webster kindly dialed it five times, so that I could take it down."

"This could be our lead then," said Calloway.

"Yes," nodded Hill, "and we can arrest Webster right away. He's ready to sign a confession."

"He's admitted everything?" asked Newton incredulously.

"Not in so many words yet, but he's given himself

away. He's definitely working with Stan Boston."

The inspector passed the crucial phone number to Newton. "Follow it up and find out all you can. It's a local London number." Then turning to Morgan and Hill, he added, "Let's have another go at Webster."

Tom Webster had not moved since Hill had left him. When he saw the three officers enter, however, he straightened his back. Before they could speak, the old crook declared, "I'll sign a confession if you promise to run in Boston and make him stand trial too!"

"But he's denied he was there," objected Hill.

"Stan Boston was there all right," laughed Webster. "The store owner identified him correctly."

Tom Webster was too lost in thoughts of revenge to notice the astonished glances that passed between Calloway and Morgan. They couldn't even begin to guess what had been said in that very room, and how Constable Leslie Hill had persuaded Tom Webster to come clean.

To the young recruit's great satisfaction, he was fully accepted from that day on as an equal partner in the Robbery Squad.

The careful reader will probably know already how Tom Webster showed that he had been lying. Or to put it another way: how did Hill guess that Webster was still very much in touch with Boston?

THE
IVORY CLOCK

It had started like any other day, that bright September morning. Nothing pointed to the terrible event that was to happen before it came to an end.

Shortly after nine o'clock, the first party of tourists arrived at the famous Belgian castle, and at 9:30 precisely, Ferdinand Muscatel, the official guide, led the first conducted tour of the day through the historic rooms of the Château Rouge. There was a great deal for visitors to see.

The walls were hung with rare tapestries, the floors were covered with silky oriental carpets. However, it was the rather uncomfortable but splendid furniture that was admired above all else. Ferdie could tell a tale about almost every single item, and the beauty of it was that no one knew for sure if he was spinning a yarn, or if the story happened to be true.

The high spot of each tour was the last room of all, the Green Drawing Room. It contained the castle's most precious treasure, a dainty mantelpiece clock, only twenty centimeters high. It was made of hand-carved ivory and it was studded all over with jewels.

In order to protect it from prying fingers, the clock was housed in a walnut cabinet. As he opened these doors, Muscatel explained how hundreds of years before, the clock had been given to the baron who owned the castle by the Empress of China who had fallen in love with him. This story was told amid admiring "Oohs!" and "Ahs!" from the tourists.

When the first tour was over, Muscatel had only a short break before the second one began at 10:30. The third followed an hour later. At 12:30, the castle gates were closed, so that the staff could have their lunch.

It was Muscatel's duty to count the visitors on their arrival, and also to make sure that all the members of each group were present and accounted for before they left. At 3 P.M. sharp, Ferdie Muscatel guided the fourth party of the day through the impressive apartments and at four o'clock, it was the turn of the fifth group to admire the treasures of the château.

The sixth and last tour of the day was scheduled for 5 P.M. As they were leaving the Green Drawing Room, Ferdinand's attention was diverted by the honking of a horn in the courtyard below, which was used as a parking lot. He looked down and saw that the driver of the bus, an old friend of his, was waving to him. He waved back cheerfully and they shouted a word or two of greeting before the guide returned to his duties.

Normally this would have been the end of Muscatel's working day and he could have gone home. At the last moment, however, a bus load of Austrian tourists showed up. They had come such a long way that Ferdinand reluctantly agreed to an extra tour, but privately he decided he would cut it short and leave out the last few rooms. When he reached the door of the Green Drawing Room, he walked straight past it without batting an eyelid.

The Austrians left the castle none the wiser and Ferdinand sighed with relief. He was about to lock the great double doors of the entrance hall when he heard a most unexpected sound: it was someone snoring.

Ten seconds later, he discovered a man who had bedded down on a half-hidden windowseat and was snoring away to his heart's content. Muscatel woke the sleeping visitor with a tap on the shoulder. The man said he was a member of the last group and admitted shamefaced that he had been unable to endure yet another conducted tour. The tour group had already been through two museums, four churches, and an art gallery.

Ferdie politely pointed out that the bus was about to leave without him. At this, the visitor's fatigue vanished. Swearing under his breath, he sprinted for the gate.

It was exactly sixty seconds too late that Ferdinand Muscatel wised up. How could this man have belonged to the Austrian group? Ferdie had counted forty-seven of them on arrival, and had said goodbye to forty-seven as they left.

Ferdinand started moving on the double. He raced up to the second floor three steps at a time. He flung open the door of the Green Drawing Room and then opened the little walnut cabinet. . . . His knees buckled, and he collapsed on a green damask stool in utter despair.

The ivory clock had been stolen!

There had been seven guided tours through the castle that day, and the thief must have mingled with one of them. Which tour was it?

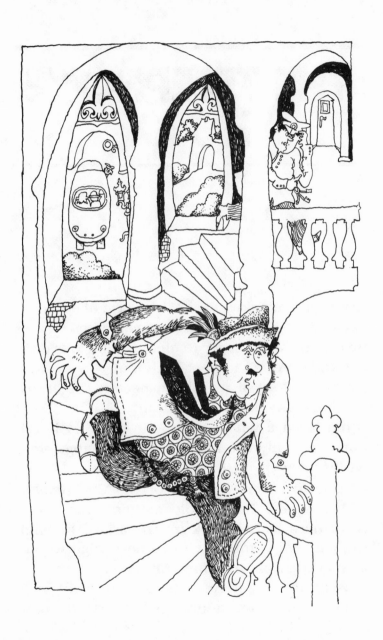

THE TELEPHONE HOAX

Arne Larsen looked for all the world like a good-natured, well-fed teddy bear. Even when he was upset, he was so eager to please that it was difficult to lose one's temper with him.

"Even if I say it myself, Inspector, I've an exceptional memory," he began. "If I had to, I could learn a whole telephone book by heart. But now I only want to forget those gangsters. I wish they were in Timbuctoo!"

Inspector Sven Christen of the Copenhagen CID nodded. "That would certainly make our work here in Denmark much easier," he said, smiling. "How long have you been nightwatchman at this coin museum, Mr. Larsen?"

"From the day it opened." Arne thought for a moment and then announced, "That was nine years, two weeks and five days ago." His right fist pounded the palm of his left hand as he added angrily, "And nothing has ever happened till now. We haven't lost a single item."

Again the inspector smiled, Sergeant Olden smiled, and even Arne Larsen himself managed a rueful half-smile.

"And last night, the whole collection disappeared in one fell swoop down to the smallest coin," the inspector stated wryly, gazing round the large circular exhibition hall with its glass-fronted showcases and cabinets. "Well, Mr. Larsen, let's have the details. A good description may help us to catch the crooks before they escape across the frontier. You mentioned you'd had a phone call. Where does that come in?"

Arne Larsen rubbed the back of his hand over his unshaven chin. "Shortly after eleven o'clock last night, I had a call from Inspector Dagerson at police headquarters."

"We've no one called Dagerson on the staff," interrupted Sergeant Olden.

"All the same, that's what he called himself," said Larsen impatiently. "And he told me he had information about a plot to break into the museum so he was sending round two officers who would be with me almost immediately."

"Didn't you suspect it might be a hoax?" asked the sergeant.

"Why should I?" retorted the nightwatchman sharply. "Would you have smelled a rat if you'd been in my position?"

"No one's blaming you, Mr. Larsen." Inspector Christen tried to calm him down. "You couldn't possibly have known the call wasn't genuine. But what happened next?"

"About five minutes later, there was a ring at the door. In the ordinary way, I wouldn't have answered it so late at night, but I was really expecting the police." Arne Larsen paused before continuing his tale. Then the words rushed out.

"When I opened up, there were seven hooligans, all masked, who pushed their way inside. I was scared out of my wits. They bolted the door and grabbed my keys. What could I do? I was one against seven. One of them stood over me with a pistol, while the others emptied the display cases and rifled the safe."

Here Arne Larsen took a deep breath, like a conjuror bracing himself to perform his most difficult trick. Full of self-importance, he addressed the two police officers.

"One wore a thick, red turtle-neck sweater and a large silver cross on a heavy silver chain. Another limped badly, dragging his left leg. I noticed he had wristwatches on both arms." At this, Larsen tapped his forehead. "Must have been a bit dotty, if you ask me," he suggested, and then carried on with his descriptions.

"A third fellow was so tall that the others called him Lofty. He talked through his nose, like someone with adenoids. Oh yes, he was the one with a bushy beard. Then there was the one in white jeans and rubber boots which were several sizes too big for him. And the chap who did most of the talking wore glasses—you could see them behind his mask. He kept egging them on:

'Hurry up boys, get a move on!' The fellow standing over me was wearing a track suit and he seemed to have a tic."

"What kind?" asked Christen.

"Like this," Larsen demonstrated, twitching his left shoulder up and down.

"I see," said the inspector.

"The lame one was very fair, his hair was almost white. He could have been Swedish, judging by his accent. The others were all dark, though. And one thing more. That red sweater I mentioned before had two white stripes round the sleeves."

"What a memory!" exclaimed the inspector. "Why, you could appear on television as the Memory Man!"

Larsen was clearly flattered. "Does my description help?" he asked, gingerly fingering the bruise on his head, the intruders' parting gift to him.

"It certainly does," Christen assured him. "I'm

sure it was the Agerstrom gang. They like hitting the headlines, so they go in for these fancy tricks."

The two policemen appeared to be completely satisfied as they left the museum. Nevertheless, there was one flaw in Larsen's account, which proves that even the best memory can sometimes let one down. If you look carefully at the picture showing the gang in action, you should be able to spot where he was wrong.

What was Larsen's mistake?

THE TELL-TALE DIARY

During the night of January 2, unknown thieves forced entry through a cellar door into the well-known beauty shop, Rigi and Eiger, in the center of Zurich, Switzerland. They got away with expensive perfumes and beauty products worth several thousand francs. On-the-spot inquiries made no headway as there were neither fingerprints nor other useful clues.

A few days later, however, an elderly lady went to the police and made the following statement:

Toward midnight on January 2, I went out to mail a letter. On my way to the main post office, I saw a young couple looking in Rigi and Eiger's main window. They were smoking, but they weren't actually speaking as I passed.

When I came back the same way about twenty minutes later, only the girl was there, standing beside a pile of suitcases, four or five, as far as I remember.

I forgot all about it until I read about the break-in in the local paper. That reminded me of what I had seen, so I thought I had better report it.

This was all the good lady had to say, but it turned out to be the first ray of light in the case of Rigi and Eiger.

At 3 P.M. that same day, the police in a market town eighty miles away phoned Zurich headquarters to say that they had picked up a young man who was trying to sell well-known French perfumes at well below their usual price. His name was Thomas Beck and he was alone. There was no girl with him.

Three hours later, Beck was driven to Zurich for further investigation. After some two hours' interrogation, Thomas Beck gave in, and at 8 P.M. he signed a confession. But—he denied stoutly that he had had a girl accomplice and nothing would budge him from his version of the robbery. Inspector Kramer who was in charge of the case had to call it a day. He gave orders for Beck to be detained and he went home in a very bad temper.

The following morning, the inspector was at his desk much earlier than usual. As soon as he had dealt with the necessary routine matters, he said to his assistant, Sergeant Werder, "Come on, Werder, let's take a look at Beck's stamping ground. I've a hunch we might discover who was working with him."

Thomas Beck lived in a hostel for young men. He seemed to be on good enough terms with the other lads there, but he had few close friends. So it took the two police officers some time before they obtained the name of Beck's most recent girlfriend, Caroline Kemp. Once they knew that, they had no difficulty in finding out her address.

It was nearly noon when Inspector Kramer and his colleague rang the bell at the flat where Caroline lived. A woman wearing an outdoor coat opened the door.

"Yes? What is it?" she asked, her eyes both suspicious and hostile.

"If you are Mrs. Kemp, we'd like a word with you," said Inspector Kramer and he told her who he was.

The hostility in Mrs. Kemp's eyes changed to serious concern. "Is it anything to do with my daughter Caroline?" she asked nervously.

The inspector replied with another question, "Isn't she in?"

Mrs. Kemp shook her head, and she was even

more upset when she learned that her daughter was under suspicion of robbery. "I simply can't believe it of her, Inspector," Mrs. Kemp shook her worried head. "And she's never mentioned anyone called Thomas Beck. She's such a good girl, really. Here! Look at this!"

Inspector Kramer took from her a piece of paper which had been lying on the table. This is what he read:

Dear Mum,
I've gone shopping. I've made you some cof-
fee and left it in the thermos bottle.
If you'd like to know what I've been doing
while you were away, you can read all
about it in my new diary. See you later.
                                    Caroline

"Has your daughter always kept a diary?" asked the inspector, handing back the note.

Mrs. Kemp didn't know what to say. "Actually, I'm a bit surprised at it. She's never kept a diary before. I suppose that since it's the new year . . . Shall I fetch it?"

"Please do."

A couple of minutes later, Mrs. Kemp returned carrying a small black notebook.

"Thank you," said the police officer and sat down to read. After a moment's glance, he said,

"I think I'll read this aloud." And he proceeded to do so:

Wednesday, December 31
My first day on my own. Mum has gone to stay with Granny. I was at work till lunch-time, then we had the half day off, so I went to the movies. (Sci-fi film—terrific!) In the evening, went to Freda's New Year's Eve party. Had a lovely time. Home at 1 A.M. after we'd seen the New Year in.

January 1
Holiday. Hurray! Slept till eleven, then made myself some soup. Wrote to Christina. In the afternoon, washed my best white lace blouse. P. and I went to a disco in the evening. Back at midnight. Rotten headache.

January 2
Headache won't go. Had to go in to work, though. Everyone upset about new insurance deductions. There won't be much left in our paychecks! After work, phoned Aunt Anna and had a nice chat. Went to bed early (9 P.M.) and read for a while.

January 3
Thank goodness for the weekend. Barbara came and we went to buy tickets for the

new ice show. Went for a long walk in the afternoon and B. came back with me (about six o'clock). We had supper and then watched "Dallas" on TV.

January 4
Spent the morning shopping. Bought bread and groceries, then to the butcher for sausages. Managed to find a matching zip at the department stores for my new yellow blouse —it's nearly finished. Had a hamburger for lunch at Pete's Bar in Station Road. Barbara and I went to a disco in the afternoon. Back home by 10 P.M.

January 5
Inspector Kramer flung the notebook on the table. "No more entries after January 5. I'm hardly surprised."

Mrs. Kemp looked at him in astonishment. "What's wrong, Inspector?" she asked, baffled. "It can all be checked, I'm sure."

"Of course," answered Kramer with a grim smile, "and most of it may be correct. But that doesn't alter the fact that this diary—if you can call it that—has been concocted to establish an alibi and mislead the police if necessary. Your daughter has made a serious mistake, Mrs. Kemp."

"What do you mean?" Mrs. Kemp sounded

choked and her hands played helplessly with Caroline's note.

Kramer pointed to the notebook. "She's handed it to us on a plate. Take a good look at what she's written. I'm sure her mistake will strike you if you re-read it carefully."

At that moment, they heard the sound of a key in the lock of the front door.

"If that's Caroline, she'll be furious with herself for giving the game away," said Inspector Kramer, sorrier for the mother than the girl.

What was Caroline's crucial mistake? Why was her diary so unconvincing to the inspector?

BLACKMAIL WITH MUSIC

It was nearly seven o'clock one Friday evening in April. Two men sat in the living room of a second floor apartment in a quiet suburb of Birmingham. One of them, a red-haired young man with horn-rimmed glasses, was puffing at a cigarette, deep in thought. The other, who was older and more relaxed, was playing the old Irish song, "The Londonderry Air" on a recorder. He played the gentle haunting tune very well indeed.

"It's more or less seven," said the young man. "I'll call him now." He stood up and went to the telephone. When the man at the other end of the line answered—"Frank Bull speaking," his face took on a sarcastic smile as he replied, "A very good evening to you, Mr. Bull!"

Dead silence.

Then Bull's voice again, this time mistrustfully: "Who's there?"

"I haven't had the pleasure of meeting you, Mr. Bull, but I want to ask you something. Are you aware of the house rules of the firm of Wicks & Wicks where you work?"

There was a faint gasp from Bull and the young man smirked all the more.

"That gave you a nasty fright, didn't it? And no wonder. You know as well as I do that anyone caught borrowing the firm's equipment will be dismissed without notice, don't you?"

"What *is* all this?" replied Bull hoarsely. "Will you kindly explain what you're talking about?"

"Of course," the voice went on. "You can't have forgotten Sebastian Penn so quickly! The poor fellow only borrowed a small dictaphone, but he got the sack the moment it came to light. And you've been even naughtier, you must admit. That electronic calculator you slipped in your case as you left the office is a very expensive one, as you know very well. Still, we don't want you to share Penn's fate, Mr. Bull, we're not hard-hearted. We'll keep quiet if you cough up a thousand pounds. You have till Sunday evening to find the cash."

"But I don't possess a thousand pounds."

"Then you'd better get busy and find it." The young man's voice had turned hard and ugly.

"How can I raise so much money so quickly?" asked Bull in despair. "It's the weekend and. . . ."

"That's your affair. I'll call again on Sunday evening with detailed instructions. One thousand pounds, or else! Good-bye!"

The red-headed young man replaced the receiver with a flourish. The older man had been playing the recorder all through the conversation, but he hadn't missed a word.

"Well, how was I?" asked the young man cockily. "You didn't know you had a budding actor in the family, did you? Your dear colleague was really shattered. . . . But I have to be off. See you on Sunday!"

Blackmail!

Shock, fear, and anger surged through Frank Bull's head as he, too, replaced the telephone. Who was behind it? Who could have known that he had borrowed the office electronic calculator to use at home over the weekend? And what could he do about the threat to his job?

A sleepless night followed that wretched Friday evening. Should he hold out—or would it be better to pay up? Yet suppose he gave in, how could he be sure that the blackmailer would leave him alone afterwards? Was this an end to his promising career with the firm of Wicks & Wicks?

It was almost dark on Saturday evening when Frank Bull remembered something. His cousin had once mentioned that a famous private detective, Bernard Martin, lived just around the corner. As soon as Frank Bull phoned him, he agreed to help. Yes, of course Mr. Bull could come round right away. No, no, it was no trouble. He was used to being called on at any hour.

Bernard Martin was a tall man in his late forties, well-groomed, confidence-inspiring.

"Come in, Mr. Bull," he greeted his visitor. "Do sit down and tell me what's the problem."

"I should first explain that I'm an accountant, Mr. Martin, and that I work for Wicks & Wicks. I expect you've heard of them."

"Oh, yes," answered Martin. "They're one of the biggest electrical engineers in the district."

"I should also explain that in my spare time, I help my brother-in-law with his accounts," Frank Bull went on. "He has his own business but he can't afford much modern equipment. So I borrowed a desk calculator from the office to use this weekend."

Bernard Martin frowned thoughtfully. "Is that allowed? Most firms, I believe, don't like it much."

"That's just the point. Wicks & Wicks are very

strict about it. It's absolutely forbidden and I've never done it before. But it saves so much time that I thought for once. . . . Now if the firm finds out, I'll be fired on the spot," confessed Frank miserably.

"You mentioned over the phone that you were being blackmailed. Is it about the calculator?"

"Yes, the man who phoned said that if I didn't pay him one thousand pounds, he'd spill the beans and I'd get the sack."

"It sounds like someone working in your department. Didn't you recognize the voice?"

"No," answered Bull slowly. "But I've just thought of something. Yesterday, as I was slipping the machine into my case, I heard someone opening my door. But no one came in. . . . And it's only now I realize how important it was."

"How do you mean, important?" asked the detective, very interested.

"Because it limits the suspects to four people. I have a small office to myself, but that particular door leads to an inner office and the four clerks who work there pass through my room every time they come and go. It must be one of them."

"Go on," Martin encouraged his visitor.

"There's something else too," said Bull pensively. "It may not be important, but during that ghastly phone call, I could hear music playing. Live music, I mean, not a radio or a record player, because it was the same song, over and over again."

"Can you say what instrument it was?"

"I'm not sure—something you blow."

"A harmonica perhaps?"

"N–n–no–but it might have been the one you learn at school. . . . What *is* its name, now? . . . the word's on the tip of my tongue."

"Do you mean a recorder?"

"That's it! Not that it helps much. I don't think I know anyone who plays one."

"It may be something to go on, all the same," said Martin. "However, I think our best bet is for me to pay these four gentlemen a visit tomorrow morning. Do you know if they live locally?"

"Yes, I think they all live quite close. I have two of their addresses, Stephen Field's and Harry Onslow's. If you'd kindly pass me the phone book, I'll probably find the others. . . . Yes, here they are, Major and Greene, all within a couple of miles. You don't know how grateful I am for your help, Mr. Martin."

Sunday morning
Bernard Martin had worked out a plan of action. Taking the farthest address first, he found himself outside the house of Mr. Gerald Greene at 10:15 precisely. Mr. Greene, a tall severe-looking

man of about thirty, opened the door to Bernard's ring.

"Yes, what is it?" he asked abruptly.

"I'd like a word with you if I may. It's about Mr. Frank Bull who works in your department. My name is Martin."

Greene looked surprised and far from friendly. "Why? Has something happened to him?" he asked coldly, as if he didn't much care if it had.

"In a way, yes," answered Bernard Martin. "You could put it like that."

"You'd better come in," said Greene after a pause. He showed his caller into the living room with obvious reluctance.

"Yes, Frank's in trouble," Martin went on. "In fact, he's being blackmailed."

"Blackmailed? You can't be serious!"

"I'm afraid I am. After work on Friday, he borrowed some office equipment to use at home over the weekend. Someone working in your inner office saw him taking it, and now that person is demanding one thousand pounds for not telling the management."

"What a low-down trick!" exclaimed Greene, flushing with what seemed real indignation this time. "I wouldn't have believed anyone would be so mean!"

"Have you any idea who's doing it?" asked the detective.

"Not at all. I can't even guess who it is."

"Are you musical, Mr. Greene?"

"What has that to do with Bull?" asked Greene, astonished. "But if you must know, the answer is I'm not. I can't even whistle." The young man smiled nervously.

"Thank you, Mr. Greene, you've been more than helpful," said Bernard, returning the smile. "I'd be grateful, however, if you said nothing to your colleagues about my visit."

"There's no fear of that, Mr. Martin. I never see them outside the office."

By now it was 10:50 and it had started to rain, so the detective was glad that his next port of call was only a few minutes away. It was Mr. Field's house, the second address on his list.

Stephen Field, who opened this door himself, was a tall thin man with a reddish nose and drooping, crinkled eyelids. "Are you collecting for charity?" he asked warily.

"No," replied Bernard, "I've come to see you about Frank Bull from your office. I'm a private detective."

"What's Bull been up to? It doesn't sound like him to need the attention of a private detective."

"Mr. Bull was thoughtless enough to borrow a piece of office equipment to use at home this weekend. As bad luck would have it, someone from the inner office where you work saw him doing it and now he's being blackmailed."

"But dash it all," Stephen Field blinked and his voice grew husky. "Surely no one would want to make trouble for Bull, even if they caught him in the act."

"I'm afraid you're wrong. Unless Bull hands over one thousand pounds, this man will go to the boss and have him sacked."

The thin man shook his head in disbelief. "No one would stoop so low as to. . . ." He stopped suddenly. "Good heavens, you don't think I. . . . Am I under suspicion too?"

"I've no idea who's the culprit, Mr. Field. Just one more question, though. Are you a musical person?"

"Yes, you might say so. I play the piano."

"Any other instruments?"

"Yes, I get by on the viola, and I'm not too bad with the clarinet. But the piano's the one. . . ."

"What about the recorder?"

"The recorder? I haven't played that since I was at school, but I think I could play it if I tried. Has it something to do with Bull?"

"Yes, it's one piece in the jigsaw, you might say. Thank you for your help, Mr. Field."

The rain was over by the time Bernard approached the third of Frank Bull's colleagues,

Harry Onslow. He turned out to be a cheerful person, younger than either Greene or Field.

"Mr. Martin, did you say? Do come in, you've just caught me. Five minutes later and you'd have found the house deserted. I was going fishing."

"I shan't keep you long, Mr. Onslow. I've come about Frank Bull, from your office."

"Frank Bull?" exclaimed Onslow. "Why didn't he come himself? He knows where I live. I hope he hasn't been taken ill."

"No, he's all right. But something happened on Friday when you were all packing up to go home. Someone in the room where you work noticed that Bull had slipped one of the firm's electronic devices into his case, so that he could do some private work on Saturday. And now, this person has put a pistol, so to speak, at Mr. Bull's head. Either he hands over one thousand pounds, or else he'll be reported to the powers-that-be."

Harry Onslow sprang to his feet and paced up and down the room, his hands clasped tightly behind his back. He seemed to be so angry that he couldn't trust himself to speak. Suddenly he turned and faced Martin. "But that's outrageous! Frank would be sacked without notice if the boss knew."

"Exactly. And that's why I'm trying to trace the blackmailer before it's too late. I don't suppose you noticed anything odd on Friday afternoon?"

"No, nothing at all. But then I sit with my back to the door and I don't see what's going on in Frank's office, not unless I turn round, that is."

"They tell me you're very musical, Mr. Onslow."

"Musical? Me?" Harry Onslow laughed at the mere idea. "They must have been pulling your leg, Mr. Martin. I can't tell 'Baa Baa Black Sheep' from 'God Save the Queen!' "

It was four minutes to twelve when the detective reached the fourth and last address on his list, a six-story block of apartments in Church Road. He took the elevator to the second floor. He had barely touched the bell before a voice called out, "Come in, Ben! It's not locked!"

"Sorry. I'm not Ben actually. . ." began Martin, stepping into the inner hall. Before he could finish his sentence, a bedroom door flew open and a man stepped into the corridor.

"I do beg your pardon—I thought it was my nephew." The apartment owner looked his caller up and down, uncertain what to make of him.

"I should be the one to apologize," replied Bernard. "You must be Mr. Max Major."

"Yes, that's right."

"My name is Bernard Martin and I'm a private detective. I've come to see you on urgent business. It's about Frank Bull, who works with you at Wicks & Wicks."

Mr. Major showed Martin into a nicely furnished living room with several roomy armchairs.

"What's up with Bull?" he asked inquisitively.

"Someone's trying to blackmail him, Mr. Major. I thought you might be able to suggest who it is."

"What's Bull supposed to have done?"

"Last Friday he was seen borrowing a piece of the firm's equipment, just as he was stowing it away in his briefcase, in fact. I'm told that Wicks & Wicks are very strict about these things. They don't allow their staff. . . ."

"You're quite right," Major interrupted, eager to have his say. "It's happened before, you know. A fellow in the next office—Sebastian something or other—did exactly the same and he was dismissed without notice. And he'd only borrowed a little pocket dictaphone, not an expensive electronic calculator. But why doesn't Bull go to the police?"

"He'd rather settle things quietly, if possible. And of course, he can still go to the police later, if he changes his mind. Can't you throw any light on what happened?"

"No," said Major after a little thought. "I can't suggest anything."

"Are you musical, Mr. Major?"

"Well, I play the guitar a bit—and the mouth

organ. And I used to sing in the choir at. . . ."

"What about the recorder?"

Major looked decidedly amused. "Why do you ask such an odd question?" he retorted.

"Oh, it's part of the routine, you know."

"Then the answer is no. Is there anything else?"

At that moment, the doorbell rang. "That'll be Ben, my nephew. He's come to fetch me for lunch. He's always in and out of my flat, drinking my Coke, you know what young people are. Ha! ha! ha!"

"Then I shan't keep you any longer, Mr. Major. Thank you for your help. Good morning!"

Frank Bull was beside himself with excitement as he ushered Bernard Martin indoors the moment the detective arrived at his house.

"I'm on pins and needles, Mr. Martin. I've been trying to get you on the phone for the past hour, but there was no reply."

"No, of course not, I've been visiting your colleagues. What's happened?"

"It's the recorder!" explained Bull excitedly. "It's been nagging away at me ever since we spoke. I felt sure it rang a bell, and now. . . ." He thrust an old photograph into Martin's hands. "See what I've found!"

The detective looked at the picture closely. "When was it taken?"

"About four years ago, when our department took a trip to Stratford-upon-Avon. Do you recognize the man at the back with the recorder? He'd only joined us recently, so I suppose I didn't take much notice of him."

Frank's hands were trembling as Bernard handed him back the photo. He glared at it with loathing.

"Yes, I do," said Martin coolly. "And I agree with you entirely. He's the blackmailer all right."

"Then what's the next move?"

The private detective smiled. "We'll wait till this evening and then we'll go and call on the gentleman in question. I think we can make him see that dabbling in blackmail is a dangerous game. At any rate, it's worth trying. . . ."

Bernard Martin, private detective, had called on four men. After speaking to each in turn, he was satisfied that one of them was responsible for trying to blackmail Mr. Bull. Which of them was responsible for that worrying and cruel telephone call at seven o'clock on Friday evening?

MRS. ANGEL— WITNESS

The thunderstorm went on for more than half an hour. It sounded as if the end of the world had come. In the darkness of the night, howling gusts of wind swept through the streets relentlessly, and everything that wasn't securely fastened was tossed into the air and came crashing down again.

It was exactly 2:32 A.M. by the church clock as Mrs. Angel turned into Quay Street, but she had hardly turned the corner before she froze in her tracks. What she had seen shocked her so much that she needed several minutes before she could go on. The howling gale tore at her head-scarf and her coat. She was trembling so hard that she feared her legs would give way. At last she got a grip on herself and looked around anxiously for someone to come to her aid. There was no one. The streets were deserted.

At last she remembered that she had passed a
pay phone not many yards back. Battling with
the wind and panting for breath, she made her
way toward it. It was an enormous relief to her

when a voice at the other end of the line answered, "Police headquarters."

Mrs. Angel stammered out a few words and the same voice replied, "Hold the line, please. I'll put you through to Inspector Quick."

Almost immediately a much deeper voice was heard. "Inspector Quick speaking. Please repeat what you just told the switchboard operator."

Without further prompting, Mrs. Angel told her story. "I've just come from the railway station, and as I turned into Quay Street, a delivery van pulled up right in front of the big fur shop. You know the one I mean, Basil Martenson. Two men jumped out of the van and the one started cutting a large hole in the main window. . . . No, I don't know what he was using—I was too far away. In fact, it gave me such a fright, I didn't know what to do. They made a clean sweep of the furs on display and piled them inside the van."

Here Mrs. Angel had to pause for breath and the inspector used the opportunity to ask hurriedly, "Where exactly are you now?"

"In the phone booth in Cross Street, just before you get to Quay Street."

"Stay right where you are. We'll be there immediately."

Mrs. Angel replaced the receiver and leaned against the wall of the phone booth. She felt exhausted.

She hadn't long to wait. In less than five minutes, a police car drew up at the curb and a police officer got out.

"I'm Inspector Quick," the stout, fatherly policeman introduced himself. "It's a pity but those self-service customers you saw must be miles away by now. All the same, I'd be glad if you could repeat your account of what you witnessed. You were coming from the station, you said?"

"Yes," nodded Mrs. Angel. "The wind was so fierce that I had to fight my way down Cross Street, and I'd just reached the corner of Quay Street when I saw the car parked outside the fur shop. Two men. . . ."

"Are you sure there were two of them?" Quick interrupted her.

"Oh, yes, there were two of them all right. But as I was saying, the storm was at its height and in fact, there was such a loud clap of thunder at that moment that I didn't actually hear them smashing the shop window. I suppose they used a brick, or something. . . . Oh, yes, and then they heaped the furs into the trunk. I was so terrified. . . ."

"Don't worry, madam. You're quite safe now. One last question, though. Can you describe the men?"

The lady thought for a moment. "One seemed much younger than the other. He had a small pinched-looking face and he wore a light-colored scarf around his neck. The other was nearly bald, but not an old man—less than forty, I'd say."

The police inspector took the woman gently by the arm and led her to the car. "You'd better come to headquarters with us, madam. Then we can go over the facts together and try to get things straight. Perhaps you'll have recovered from your shock and you'll be able to remember exactly what you witnessed. I'm afraid it's rather a muddle so far. We'll need a formal statement, and it had better be accurate."

Mrs. Angel stared at the inspector, bewildered. "But I've already told you all I saw!"

"Yes, but what you said on the phone is different in three important respects from what you told me just now."

What are the three contradictions in Mrs. Angel's statements?

THE BLACKOUT

Seventy-year-old Alfred Simpkins had been looking forward all day to that evening's viewing on TV. There was to be a repeat of an exciting thriller, "The Stowaway," which he had missed the first time around. It was to be at 8:30, and Alfred switched on in very good time.

You can imagine his disappointment, then, when at 8:28 it was announced that "The Stowaway" had been rescheduled for the following evening. Instead, there would be a live broadcast from the European Horse Show Jumping competition. Poor Mr. Simpkins! He hated show jumping. Disgruntled, he took himself off to bed.

He didn't find out till the next day that he couldn't have watched the film, even if it had not been cancelled. For no sooner had he switched off his bedroom light than there was a blackout.

The electricity supply failed and the town was left in darkness. The technicians got to work immediately, but in spite of their efforts, they did not find the fault until ten o'clock. They discovered that the installation had been sabotaged. Someone who must have known his way around a power station had deliberately damaged the main supply.

At about the same time, the police were informed that, under cover of total darkness, the two biggest jewelry shops in the town had been burglarized. The Robbery Squad was convinced that Jack Carpenter, a well-known crook, had been at work. Before taking up a life of crime, he had been employed at the power station, which was close to where he lived.

Soon after midnight, two police officers arrived at Carpenter's house and got him out of bed. Jack protested that he had a complete alibi. From 8:30 till 10:00, he had been watching a whodunit on TV, "The Stowaway." He could even tell them the plot and which actors had taken part. The police laughed heartily. Carpenter of all people should have known this was a lie, because of the failure of the electricity supply.

"So what?" retorted Carpenter, laughing in his turn. "I don't need electricity to watch TV. Mine runs on batteries! See for yourselves."

Nevertheless, the police had the last laugh. Battery TV or regular TV was beside the point. The Robbery Squad had no difficulty in proving that Carpenter's alibi was a false one, and he was promptly arrested.

How did the police prove that Jack Carpenter's alibi couldn't have been genuine?

THE
TERRIBLE TWINS

He loomed in the doorway like an enormous stone statue, tall, broad-shouldered and heavy-set. "Are you Baldwin Puff, the detective?" he thundered.

I hastily swallowed the last mouthful of fish and chips I'd been having for my supper. "Yes," I mumbled, "that's me."

"Good," nodded the man at my door. "I'd like a word with you." The statue edged its bulk indoors and I had to pull in my stomach to let it pass. Even Chippie, my dachshund, was so impressed by the size of the man's feet that he didn't risk the faintest growl.

"My name is Nick Nicholas," bellowed the visitor, his voice filling the entire room.

"Please take a seat, sir," I said with a sickly smile, trembling for the springs of my poor armchair beneath his tremendous weight.

"If it's all the same to you, I'd rather stand." Mr.

Nicholas leaned against the wall and I could hear it groaning.

"I'll not beat about the bush, Mr. Puff. It's about my two nephews, my sister's boys. They've been staying with me during the school holidays, and they've been getting on my nerves all week, I can tell you. To top it off, I discovered yesterday that my gold cigarette lighter and heavy gold chain are missing."

Before I could get a word in, he glared at me so severely, I began to wonder if I myself were the thief, but soon his voice boomed out again. "I couldn't have lost them, because I keep them firmly attached to the vest of my brown suit which hangs at the back of my closet. In any event, it's nearly a month since I last wore it, long before Peter and Paul arrived."

Timidly I asked the most obvious question. "Have you spoken to the boys?"

"There's no point. If I got over-excited, I might lose my temper and hit them—with this!" He held out his massive fist. "Look at the size of it, man!"

"It's more like a shovel than a hand, I agree," I admitted honestly. I'd never seen such a large hand before.

"If this hand strikes, it will leave a mark for life," confessed Nick Nicholas. "My dear sister would never forgive me."

"I see your problem," I nodded. "How old are your nephews?"

"One is twelve, the other thirteen."

"Who is more likely to have done it, or were the pair of them involved?"

"That's for you to find out, Mr. Puff. My car is outside. Let's go and clear the matter up without delay."

As I slipped on my jacket, I inquired, "Did they know about the lighter, and how it was secured?"

"I certainly didn't tell them, and as I said before, I haven't worn the suit since they came. Nor have they any business snooping around my bedroom."

Peter and Paul were watching television as Uncle Nick and I entered the living room. We had prepared a plan of action on our way. Accordingly, Mr. Nicholas took Paul, the taller of the two, by the scruff of the neck and marched him into the kitchen.

"I'm a detective," I announced to Peter, whose eyes showed that he was a little scared. "Have you any idea why I'm here?"

"Not the foggiest," he said, rapidly recovering from his fright.

"Your uncle has lost a valuable possession. It's been missing since yesterday."

"Really?" said Peter, as if genuinely surprised.

"You've no idea what might have happened to it?"

"I haven't a clue! What is it, by the way?"

"A gold cigarette lighter."

"He hasn't mentioned it. Why didn't he tell us? We'd have helped him look for it."

"I couldn't say."

"Are you a real detective?"

"Yes, I even have a tracker dog. You haven't found it, by any chance?"

"Your tracker dog?"

"Not Chippie—the lighter, of course."

"No. I don't smoke. What's more, I haven't been near his closet, either, word of honor."

"How about Paul?"

"He's innocent too."

"Well, we'll soon see," said I, grinning cheerfully. And Peter grinned back across his cheeky freckled face.

We exchanged nephews. Paul bounced in, beaming all over. "Uncle Nick tells me you're a Private Eye."

"Has he also told you why I'm here?"

"No. He said you'd better explain. He's in a rotten mood, these days!"

"Why would that be, do you think?"

"Dunno. Perhaps we make too much noise."

"I'm here because there's something missing."

"Oh, no! What is it, or aren't you allowed to say?"

"It's his cigarette lighter. He thinks that one of you swiped it."

"That's awful!" Paul sounded both surprised and hurt that his uncle could think so badly of him. "How can he suspect his own nephews? Would you do that, Mr. Detective?"

"I haven't any nephews."

"But if you had—?"

"Look here! I'm the one to do the questioning, not you, young man!"

"But I'm very upset. It's a dreadful thing to do, isn't it?"

"Do you mean to say that neither you nor Peter had anything to do with it?"

"That's right, that's just what I mean. I haven't been near Uncle's bedroom, and neither has my brother. I'd have been sure to know about it if Peter had gone in. Anyway, what use is a cigarette lighter to us? We don't smoke!"

"That's a good question," I answered calmly. "In fact, we'd better start trying to answer it, all of us. Don't you think it's about time?"

Who was the culprit, Paul or Peter? Or were they hand in glove?

RENT-A-GHOST

Castle Dunstan was in Yorkshire, a beautiful Tudor building set in a splendid park. When it became too expensive for its owners to maintain, they sold it to an international group. Completely modernized with dining rooms and bathrooms galore, it was transformed into the five-star luxury Castle Dunstan Hotel. It was officially opened on July 1.

The new manager was Sir John Danburgh, a full-blooded aristocrat who gave the right tone to the new hotel. He was a man of ideas as well. What better way to attract visitors, he thought, than to announce that the castle was haunted! And just to make sure that it was, and that his guests got their money's worth for the high prices charged, he hired three students on vacation to dress up as the castle's ghosts. They would be required to haunt the corridors and stairs between midnight and 1 A.M.

Catherine McKie was decked out in an ivory silk dress, one actually worn by Lady Melinda Callaway two hundred years earlier. Peter Rule, in emerald-green velvet, became the seventeenth-century Philip, Earl of Horsley, and Robert Foster, splendid in red brocade and gold, took on the role of the wicked baron, Lord Hugo Meeds, suspected of murdering his wife in 1777.

Thus the opening season began. For nine nights, the three students enjoyed themselves tremendously. In their ghostly attire, they sent delighted shivers down the spines of the hotel guests, who glimpsed them only from a safe distance. It was all good fun, and no one took it too seriously.

Not until July 10, that is, at 12:50 A.M. It was then that Mrs. Woodmaker from Chicago, Illinois, discovered her jewel case had been rifled. A diamond necklace with matching earrings had vanished into thin air. And to think she had been chatting away and laughing with Mrs. Cleopatra Kay, another lady from Chicago, while the thief was in her bedroom!

Fuming with rage, Mrs. Woodmaker summoned the manager to her room. She knew that he was still up at this late hour, for he had told her it was then that he had time to see to his accounts.

Ten minutes elapsed before poor Sir John could get a word in, but in that period, he discovered that the lady who had been robbed believed one of the ghosts was to blame for the theft.

Sir John Danburgh picked up the phone.

"Oliver speaking," the night porter answered.

"Oliver, find the three ghosts at once and bring them to my office personally," thundered the irate manager. He then asked Mrs. Woodmaker to be good enough to wait until he had interviewed the chief suspects.

Back in his room, Sir John had to be patient another seven minutes before Mr. Oliver ushered in the three students. Their faces showed nothing more than surprise and curiosity.

"What's happened?" asked Jack Oliver, obviously concerned.

"There's a thief among us, Oliver, and he—or she—has already struck."

"That's terrible!" exclaimed the night porter. "Did Mrs. Woodmaker recognize the culprit?"

Sir John pointed to the ghosts. "She's quite convinced it was one of our ghosts."

The three young people were appalled, but Peter Rule was the first to recover from the shock. He stepped forward smartly. "I demand that you inform the police at once, Sir John."

"I'd prefer the affair to be cleared up without any fuss," replied Sir John, gently but firmly.

Turning to the porter, he said, "You were on duty, Oliver. Didn't you notice anything?"

Jack shook his head. "No, nothing. I haven't left the front hall all evening. But I did happen to observe that Mr. Foster was the first to come downstairs when I called them at your request, Sir John."

"What are you suggesting?" shouted Foster indignantly. "You ought to know that my room happens to be nearest to the hall!"

Catherine McKie raised her hand timidly like a shy schoolgirl. "Why must it have been one of us, Sir John? Perhaps the lady was mistaken. . . . Isn't it possible that someone else was the thief?"

Sir John's eyes darted round the room and all at once, his face registered a mixture of alarm and disbelief. Then he turned gravely to Miss McKie. "You're quite right, young lady. The ghosts are innocent. It was a member of our own staff."

Turning swiftly to the night porter, he barked, "Well, Oliver, where have you hidden Mrs. Woodmaker's diamonds?"

The night porter almost collapsed with shock, he was so unprepared for the accusation. "W–w–why–m–m–me?" he stammered, his rosy cheeks fading to a greenish yellow. "Why are y–y–you accusing me?"

"You've given yourself away," said Sir John

curtly, "and I imagine you'll have long enough in jail to work out for yourself how you betrayed your guilt. Come on now, where is the jewelry?"

With shaking hands and drooping shoulders, Jack Oliver fished a small leather bag from a back pocket. Then pale and tottering, he staggered from the office.

"What was his mistake?" asked Catherine quietly.

"I'll tell you soon, my dear," said Sir John. "But first I must take these diamonds back to Mrs. Woodmaker."

At first sight, this looks like an easy case, but perhaps it isn't so straightforward. Do you know how Jack Oliver gave the game away?

GERANIUMS FOR POLLY

Ernie Gable adored his battered old Volkswagen beetle. He had even given it the nickname "Polly." It was past midnight one fine Friday in August, and Ernie was driving home. With a hideous roar from the rusty exhaust, the car screeched to a halt in front of the six-story apartment house where he lived. He was in luck! There was actually room to park overnight below his own living room window.

Ernie was in high spirits. He had just won the weekly bowling contest. It was the first time he'd come out on top in the bowling league, and tonight the competition had been very strong. He'd shown them! There'd be no more snickers from the older bowlers, or remarks like "Come back when you're a big boy, Ernie!" Now they had to admit he could hold his own with the best of them.

The young man locked the car carefully and looked up, wondering who was still awake. There was a light burning in the apartment on the sixth floor where he lived with his parents. Aunt Jane and Uncle Sam must still be with them, playing cards as usual.

He could see other lights too, on the fourth floor, for example, and also on the third floor where the windows were wide open. So were those on the fifth floor, but that particular apartment was in darkness. The blind was down on the second floor and no light showed from the ground floor apartment, although here again the windows were ajar. It was a warm night, with very little breeze.

Ernie was putting his key into the front door lock when something made him jump. There was a great thud, followed immediately by a tremendous shattering noise. It didn't take him long to realize what had happened. Someone had deliberately taken a large flowerpot, plant and all, and thrown it down below, so that it would land on poor Polly's roof. When Ernie had cleared away the broken fragments, the soil, and what remained of the geraniums, the dent turned out to be even worse than he had feared. It would cost him a small fortune to have it fixed.

Livid with rage, Ernie Gable looked up once more at the windows of the six apartments, one above the other. It didn't take him long to figure out from which window the flowerpot had been thrown.

Now, Supersleuths, can you tell from the illustration where the unwelcome present of flowers came from? If you study the picture carefully, you should be able to say on what floor the culprit lived.

PAUL CRABBE
IS MISSING

Send for Perry Clifton!

It was just after three o'clock on a fine Sunday in June that Perry Clifton, the famous private detective, rang the doorbell at 15 Holland Square, Mayfair, London. He was shown into a spacious private office on the ground floor, which was simply but expensively furnished.

Two men rose as Clifton entered. The elder, white-haired and keen-eyed, held out his hand first. "Mr. Clifton, I presume."

"That's right."

"I'm Christopher Boone who called you this morning. May I introduce Gerry Browne, my colleague?"

Browne was a well-built young man, whose steady gray eyes were as penetrating as those of his chief.

"Do sit down, Mr. Clifton, and I'll explain why it is I'm spoiling your Sunday afternoon," Boone began. "This is my head office and perhaps you know that although we're only a small firm, we handle the most advanced electronic inventions to be found anywhere in the world. We enjoy an international reputation and until six years ago, we worked as a fine team."

There was a pause and Clifton murmured encouragingly, "I understand. Please tell me what happened."

"We couldn't go wrong, it seemed, until Paul Crabbe, my right-hand man, became a missing person. He seemed to vanish into thin air. I was abroad when the news broke, so I flew straight back, only to have my worst fears confirmed. There was 50,000 pounds sterling missing from the safe, but more serious still, details of our very latest top secret inventions were also missing. These losses cost us millions, Mr. Clifton, for we had to go back to square one and start all over again."

"Could no one trace this Mr. Crabbe?" asked Perry.

"No. Scotland Yard worked very hard, but they found nothing. The man had disappeared from the face of the earth."

"Who had keys to the safe?" Perry wanted to know.

"Only Crabbe and I—no one else," Boone assured him.

"Could Crabbe have been persuaded to steal the papers and then have been murdered?"

"It was considered as a possibility, but it was highly unlikely. Besides, it was plain from a search of his house that he had cleared out, lock, stock, and barrel. And you'll be interested to know that our inventions keep turning up on other people's equipment. One of prime importance was discovered only last month, suitably adapted, on an ingenious computer manufactured in the Far East. . . . But now it's Gerry's turn. Let him bring you up to date."

Browne cleared his throat, his face tense with excitement. "I've just come back from Edinburgh, Scotland, where something very odd occurred. I was walking along Princes Street yesterday when out of the blue I heard a most familiar voice. I was so surprised that I stood rooted to the spot. A couple of men were talking quite loudly. One was short and fat, a complete stranger to me. But the other, the tall one. . . . I'd take my oath that he was speaking with Paul Crabbe's voice."

Here Gerry Browne took a deep breath and continued, "I couldn't make out what they were saying, although I caught the name Stokes once or twice. The little man had a Scottish accent, but the other was certainly English. I'd have sworn it was Crabbe—I could feel it in my bones."

"Didn't you actually recognize him, then?"

"At first, I saw only the two reflections in a shop window," Browne went on more slowly. "But then the taller man turned in my direction, as you do when you catch sight of someone you know unexpectedly. And automatically, I turned too, so that our eyes met. But the face was not Crabbe's. I'd never seen it before, I'm sure of that."

"What about his general appearance?"

"That fitted perfectly—Paul's height and build, his age, his walk, everything."

"And the other man? Short and fat, you said, I think?"

"Yes, a little chap. Crabbe towered over him. I didn't take much notice of him, I'm afraid. I've an idea he was wearing glasses."

"Clean-shaven?"

"Now you mention it, he may have had a beard. He struck me as being well turned out, a dapper little man, I'd say."

"What happened next?"

"They walked away and they must have taken a side turning, for when I followed, they were nowhere to be seen. But I was so convinced it was Crabbe that although I had planned to stay in Scotland till Tuesday, I returned to my hotel, packed my things, and got the next train back to London. I got in fairly late, but first thing this morning, I phoned Christopher. The rest you know. But the more I think of it, the surer I am that he must have had his face altered. It sounds like a tall story, I admit, but that person I saw in Princes Street yesterday was either Crabbe—or his ghost!"

"There are plastic surgeons who can work near miracles, I believe," said Clifton thoughtfully. "It's certainly not impossible that Crabbe had his face changed beyond recognition. One last question, Mr. Browne. Do you always use the same hotel in Edinburgh?"

It was Boone who answered. "Yes, we always send our staff to the Glengarry."

"That's right," Gerry confirmed. "That's where I stayed."

"Would Crabbe have known this hotel too?"

"Oh, yes. He always stayed there when he went to Scotland for the firm," said Christopher Boone. "But will you take the case, Mr. Clifton? Will you go to Edinburgh for me while the trail's still warm?"

"You realize there's precious little to go on, but all the same, I'll do my best. I'll see my contact at Scotland Yard tomorrow and fly north on Tuesday. Meanwhile, it would be a big help if you could let me have a photograph of Paul Crabbe as he was when he worked here. That's all I need for the moment."

A needle in a haystack

On Tuesday, June 30, the scheduled flight from Heathrow landed at Edinburgh's Turnhouse Airport at 9:15 A.M. Perry Clifton was one of the passengers. He took a taxi into Edinburgh and checked in at the Glengarry Hotel, where he had already reserved a room.

As soon as he had unpacked, Clifton went down to the reception desk to see the clerk. Perry was in luck, for it was the same Mr. Cox who had been on duty when Gerry Browne left so unexpectedly the previous Saturday.

"Of course I remember Mr. Browne, sir. Regular client of ours, Mr. Browne is."

"In strict confidence, can you tell me if anyone asked for him after he'd gone?"

"Funny you should ask," answered Mr. Cox, swiftly pocketing the five pound note that Perry Clifton had slipped into his hand. "A gentleman rang about six in the evening. Seemed most put out when he heard Mr. Browne had left."

"But you didn't actually see him, I suppose?"

"In fact I did. He turned up in person half an hour later, to make quite sure there was no mistake, he said. It was so disappointing to have missed an old friend by an hour or two. Gave his name as Haldane."

"Can you describe him?"

"A little man, on the plump side, but a snappy dresser, if you'll pardon the expression, sir. Oh yes. He wore gold-rimmed spectacles."

"Did he have a beard?"

"That's right, sir. A pointed beard and a mustache."

"An Edinburgh man, would you say?"

"No mistake about that! His accent, you know."

"Thank you for being so helpful, Mr. Cox. And not a word about this to anyone, if you don't mind. I'm sure you understand."

Perry Clifton's next appointment was at police headquarters. Commissioner Charlton, Perry's friend at Scotland Yard, had already informed Detective Inspector Joe Maclaren to expect the London detective and he was waiting to greet him.

Joe and Perry got along well from the start. Clifton rapidly went over the story of Crabbe's disappearance and Gerry Browne's strange meeting in Princes Street. He also mentioned the second man, the mysterious Mr. Haldane.

"Hm," said Joe Maclaren, a burly cheerful man in his thirties. "We've mighty little to go on—no more than a voice, when you come to think of it, and what's more, one remembered from six years ago. Now if only we'd a tape, or a few fingerprints."

Perry flicked through his notebook. A word he had underlined on the second page caught his attention. "Does the name of Stokes mean anything to you?"

The effect of the question was electric. "Stokes, did you say? Jamie Stokes?" Maclaren could hardly believe his ears.

Clifton was cautious. "I've no information about the man's first name. All I know is that the name cropped up once or twice in the conversation Gerry Browne overheard. I gather you have someone in mind."

"And how!" Maclaren laughed harshly. "He's known to the police, but he's such a slippery customer that we've never been able to catch him. He calls himself a financial consultant, but that's putting it politely. He's into every shady business deal north of the Border, provided there's enough money to be made out of it. Whenever we think we have some real evidence to put him behind bars, he whisks the main witnesses out of the country."

"It could be someone else, though. Stokes isn't such an uncommon name. . . ."

"No, Perry, if there's big money in it, some major breakthrough in computer technology for instance, it'll be 'our' Stokes, you can be sure.

If you could help us to get a watertight case against him, we'll see what we can do to trace Crabbe. I'll have a word with the Chief as soon as he's free. Mind you, Stokes is our only hope. Otherwise, we're looking for a needle in a haystack!"

The man named Stokes

Next morning, a delighted Joe Maclaren told Clifton the good news. "We've been given the green light!" he chuckled. "Stokes' telephone is being tapped and a watch kept on his house. I suggest you call on him without delay."

Soon after ten o'clock, Perry Clifton stood outside an elegant house in one of Edinburgh's fine old squares. "I've just arrived from Paris," he told the butler who answered the door. "Tell Mr. Stokes I must see him urgently. There's no time to lose. Clifton's my name, Perry Clifton."

Two minutes later, he and Stokes stood face to face. The latter was a well-groomed athletic fifty-year-old. He waved his visitor to an armchair in an overfurnished study, full of the latest office gadgetry. "I'm surprised you bring me hot news from Paris, Mr. Clifton," said Stokes. "I've no business interests there at present."

"My message is from a man who says he owes you a good turn," replied Perry coolly. "I can't tell you his name, but he wants to warn you about another man, whose name is unknown even to him."

Stokes looked more puzzled than worried. "This is all very vague. Do you know either of these names, or won't you say?"

"Unfortunately I don't, but this may help." Without hurrying, Perry took a wallet from his inner pocket and handed Stokes a snapshot.

Stokes could not conceal his curiosity and almost snatched it from Perry's hand. Clifton, his eyes glued to the other's face, did not miss the fleeting shock that Stokes betrayed. "I'm so sorry," said the financier icily, immediately recovering his poise. He handed back the picture. "I don't know the fellow from Adam."

Clifton stood up. "I've done all I can," he said indifferently. "The ball's in your court now."

"One moment!" cried Stokes, rising too. "Can't you at least say what it is I have to fear from the man in the photograph?"

"There was no word about that. My informant thought you'd know."

Joe Maclaren was waiting for Perry in an unmarked police car two streets away. "You must have frightened him out of his wits!" smiled Joe.

"Do you mean there's already been some movement?" asked Clifton.

Maclaren pointed to the telephone in the car.

"Headquarters called me to say that the moment you left, Stokes dialed a local number. He sounded very excited."

"What did he say?"

"Only that he was coming around at once to see the man he called. In fact, he's already on his way and our chaps are tailing him. We'll soon know where he's gone. Did the photo work?"

"Like magic," laughed Perry. "He declared he didn't know the man at all, but he was clearly shattered. He may be a financial wizard but he's a rotten actor."

At that moment the phone rang. After Joe had spoken for a few moments, he replaced the receiver and turned to Perry.

"What do you know!" he exclaimed. "Jamie Stokes has arrived at a private clinic a couple of miles away. They specialize in plastic surgery and can give you a brand new face, if you can pay the bill, that is."

"Shall we join him?"

"Why not?" Joe agreed. "Once we've seen the place from the outside, we can decide on our next move. Okay?"

"Okay!"

The clinic

The detective and the police inspector were screened behind a row of bushes in the park surrounding the grand three-story mansion, which was now a private hospital. Its owner and chief surgeon was Dr. Donald Dorset. A dozen cars or more were standing in the parking lot to the right of the house.

"Do you see that green Alfa Romeo? It's Stokes' car. He and Dorset must be hand in glove."

Two men emerged from the house, deep in conversation. They paused at the top of the steps.

"You know the one on the right is Stokes, don't you?" whispered Perry. "Who's the other?"

"I've never seen him before," answered Maclaren.

It was four or five minutes before the two men parted, and each went to his own car. Stokes jumped into the green Alfa and drove off so furiously that the gravel spurted under his tires.

"Let's call on Dr. Dorset," suggested Perry. "Perhaps he can tell us something."

As he and Joe moved toward the house, the second man, evidently in less of a hurry, climbed into a gleaming brown Bentley. He followed in Stokes' wake down the drive and out of the grounds.

The receptionist in nurse's uniform had disappointing news. "I'm afraid you've just missed Dr. Dorset," she said. "Didn't you see a brown

Bentley leaving? He has a consultation near Glasgow at midday."

"When will he be back?" Joe wanted to know.

"Sometime tonight, I imagine. He starts early in the day, you know. He sees the patients on his rounds at eight in the morning and operates at 9:30 punctually."

"Thanks very much, nurse. We'll look in again tomorrow."

The following morning, at 7:40, Maclaren and Perry announced themselves as police officers and were shown into Dr. Dorset's office. Dr. Dorset was scanning an X-ray photograph against a lighted screen. "I won't be a moment," he explained. "I hope it won't take long for me to confirm the identity you mentioned. My day begins at eight, you know."

"What we want to know is why you fitted out this person with a new face," said the inspector bluntly. And he flourished Crabbe's picture in front of the plastic surgeon.

Dr. Dorset took it gingerly. His hands were not quite steady. "Oh, you mean Thomas Chivers," he said after the merest glance.

"So that's what he called himself!" said Maclaren. "And why would our friend Chivers want a new face?"

Dorset raised his eyebrows. "I suppose he dis-

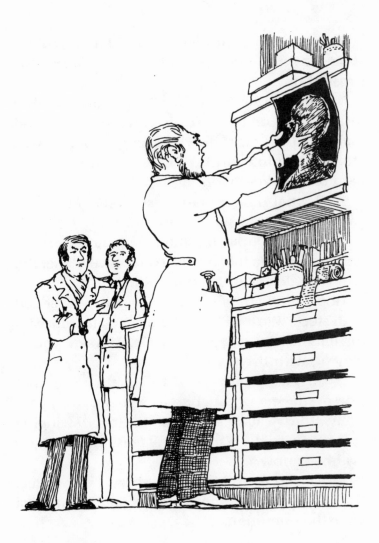

liked the old one. Most of my patients are simply dissatisfied with the way they look. It's not my business to ask them why."

"About your visitor yesterday, Jamie Stokes. What has he to do with all this!" the inspector pressed on.

The surgeon swallowed hard, uncertain whether to speak up or to bluff his way out. He stared blankly at his visitors. Then he gave in. "It was Stokes who introduced Chivers to me, and he paid for the operation."

"And what did he want yesterday?" Maclaren continued ruthlessly.

Once more Dorset hesitated and once more his nerve gave. "He took away Tom Chivers' file, the one with details of his operation."

"Good enough." Maclaren's voice was edged with steel. "We'll be back if we need any more information. But be careful, Dr. Dorset, you're playing with fire!"

As the two men turned to go, they saw that Dorset's face was as white as a sheet.

"By the way," snapped Clifton, swinging around abruptly. "Can't you at least tell us where Crabbe is now?"

Dorset shook his head. "I'm sorry, I've no idea. He said he might emigrate to South America after the operation."

"Stokes must have a stranglehold on Dorset," remarked Perry as soon as he and Joe were out of earshot. They walked thoughtfully toward the police car.

"And of course he knows Tom Chivers' real identity," the inspector added. "He must be a worried man right now. He'll cooperate with us, when the time comes—you mark my words!"

A plump little man with glasses

There was a round-the-clock watch on Jamie Stokes' house. His phone was tapped and everyone who came to see him was photographed. The police didn't have to wait long for the hoped-for breakthrough. It came on the following day.

After an early lunch, Clifton had gone to Maclaren's office. He was examining a set of prints processed that very morning by the photographic laboratory.

"Hey, look at this!" he cried suddenly. "You said you'd drawn a blank in trying to find that fellow Haldane, didn't you? Well, here's our plump friend in person, beard, glasses and all! Are you having him followed?"

"Yes. Everyone visiting Stokes is automatically shadowed."

"Then find out quickly where he is now. I'll dash back to the Glengarry and check with Mr. Cox that he's the one who asked for Browne on Saturday. I'll call you from there and you can tell me where to run him down."

Enrico's was one of Edinburgh's smartest and most expensive restaurants. By 2:25 P.M., most of the customers had finished eating, but a few lingered over their lunch. One was a plump well-dressed gentleman, whose description fitted perfectly with that of Haldane. No one shared his table.

Perry Clifton, with a scarcely audible "May I?," slipped into the seat next to him and buried himself in the enormous menu. The other was so absorbed in a monster helping of raspberries, ice cream and chocolate sauce that he hardly noticed the newcomer.

From behind the menu, with lips that barely moved, Clifton addressed his neighbor. "Don't draw attention to yourself, but listen carefully.

Stokes has just found out that Dr. Dorset has cracked. He's spilled the beans about Chivers. The police know everything."

The raspberries rolled off Haldane's spoon. He stared at Perry, mouth agape.

"Pull yourself together, man!" hissed Clifton.

"I wonder how much Dr. Dorset really knows," muttered Haldane uneasily. "It was only afterwards that we changed Chivers into Calder, wasn't it? By the way, who are you? I don't remember seeing you before."

Delighted as he was to find that Crabbe had changed his name yet again, Perry managed to hide his feelings. "I'm Clifton, the guy for special assignments," he replied, poker-faced.

Haldane showed signs of ever-growing alarm. "Has Stokes phoned Calder yet? He'll have to alert him without delay."

"But not by phone, you fool. Stokes' phone is being tapped. You'll have to warn him personally. Don't waste time, but go now. You have your car, haven't you?"

"Yes, in the parking lot here. But you can't mean that I'm to drop everything and drive to Aberdeen? . . . Oh well, if I must, I must. I'll ring Stokes. . . ."

"Idiot! Don't contact Stokes on any account, either personally or by phone, for at least four weeks. Is that clear?"

"But what about the Koreans and the new hardware? We meet them the day after tomorrow, and. . . ."

"Leave them to Stokes! Is everything clear? Good. I'll be off then!"

The hunting lodge

At 7 P.M. that same evening, a white Alfa Romeo drew up in front of an old hunting lodge not far from Aberdeen. The driver, the car's only occupant, was clearly no stranger to the servant who opened the door.

"Good evening, sir. Mr. Calder is in the study. I'll tell him you're here."

"Don't bother, William. I'll announce myself."

The master of the house looked up in astonishment as he recognized his visitor. "You, Stokes? And without letting me know in advance? What's wrong? Have the Koreans called it off at the last moment?"

"No, no. They're eating out of our hand. But I'm worried, Crabbe. . . ."

"Calder, if you don't mind!"

"Oh, William can be trusted," Stokes went on impatiently. "Yesterday, I had a mysterious visitor, a man named Clifton. He'd come from Paris, so he said, to warn me about danger from a certain quarter. It was all very vague, but he had a photo of the man who was threatening me." Stokes paused and looked the other man straight in the eye. "It was a photo of you, when you still went by the name of Paul Crabbe."

Crabbe's jaw tightened as Stokes went on, "But there's worse to come. Since then, the police have covered my every move. And they've got at Dr. Dorset too. I really think you'd better go abroad for a while."

"We've had this out before," replied Crabbe firmly. "I'm not leaving!"

"But this time, my safety's at risk, as well as yours," answered Stokes calmly.

Crabbe sprang to his feet. "If the police are shadowing you, how is it you're here now?" he asked angrily.

"They think I'm still at home. My green Alfa's in front of the house. They don't know about the white one, or my secret garage with an underground exit."

"But why are the police after you?"

"I haven't a clue. Nor do I know how they've managed to connect us. I thought we'd covered our tracks thoroughly."

The study door opened for the second time. Three pairs of eyes looked from one to the other incredulously.

"What the devil, Winston. . . . Why aren't you in Edinburgh?" barked Stokes.

Lionel Winston, *alias* Haldane, felt a clutch of

fear in the pit of his stomach. "But–but–" His arm rose feebly and his finger pointed at Stokes. "But you were the one who insisted I come here in person to warn Calder!"

"What's all this nonsense?" Crabbe rapped out, looking from one to the other.

"Why didn't you say you were being watched by the police when I saw you this morning?" Winston reproached Stokes peevishly.

"Damnation! That's my business, not yours!"

"Well, why did you give Clifton instructions to come here?" persisted Lionel.

"Clifton again!" Stokes exploded. "The man from Paris!"

"So it was Clifton who ordered you to come here to warn me?" asked Crabbe.

The lump in Winston's throat made it difficult for him to speak. "D–d–didn't you s–s–send him, Jamie?" he choked.

"Where did he find you? At your house? You said you were going straight home to lunch when you left me."

"I changed my mind," muttered Winston. "I felt like going to Enrico's instead."

"You and your fancy lunches!" sneered Stokes. "You're like a child at the thought of food. . . . You should have suspected it was a trap from the word go!"

Before Lionel could defend himself, the door was flung open with a flourish. In marched Perry Clifton and Joe Maclaren, together with Detective Inspector Crawford from the Aberdeen CID.

Winston's mouth sagged. "B–b–but, that's Clifton!" he gasped.

Maclaren stepped forward. "You are all under arrest!" he informed the astonished trio. "And here is my warrant to have the house searched!"

Epilogue

The Aberdeen home of Paul Crabbe, *alias* Chivers, *alias* Calder was searched. The papers relating to the inventions Crabbe had stolen from Christopher Boone & Co. were found in a safe. Some had already been converted into hard cash, thanks to the help of the financial wizard, Jamie Stokes. The one due to be sold to the Koreans was saved, just in time.

Lionel Winston was a lawyer. He was a vain and greedy man who did not earn enough honestly for his very expensive tastes, so that he allowed himself to be "bought" by Stokes to manipulate the legal side of the financier's shady business deals.

Dr. Donald Dorset, too, had been bribed by Stokes to alter the appearance of wanted criminals, and then blackmailed to get more deeply involved. In the end, he offered himself as a witness for the prosecution, as Maclaren had predicted, when the guilty men were brought to trial a few months later.

There are two questions to be answered:

1. Clever as Dr. Dorset was as a surgeon, he made a foolish slip. How did he betray the fact that he knew more than he had admitted?

2. Why should Lionel Winston have known that Perry Clifton's story wasn't genuine?

SOLUTIONS

The Midnight Chess Game, *page 5*

If Felix had been innocent, he would not have known that the Richard Morgan who was burgled was a fellow chess player.

The Flat Tire, *page 17*

The man with the burst tire said that he hadn't heard the radio that morning and that he knew nothing about a bank robbery. Yet it was he who mentioned that it had taken place in Assisi, something he could not possibly have guessed unless he had been involved.

The Joyride, page 22

It was Leo Sixten who was the more likely to have "borrowed" the professor's car for a joyride.

We know that he was interviewed by the inspector well after 5:30 A.M., which was the time Orndal called on Professor Berg.

If he had been telling the truth when he said he'd returned from a three-hour walk only five minutes before, how could he have known that his brother had come home "shortly after five"?

At Dead of Night, page 29

Dr. Oscar Grey told Inspector Riley that he had never heard of Jason Fry. In that case, how could he have known that he was a forger of credit cards?

The Roland Square Mystery, page 36

Webster had insisted all along that it was five years ago in Sheffield that he had last seen Stan Boston. Was it likely then that he would have known the other's telephone number so well that he didn't need to look it up? Also, he dialed a local London number, not a long-distance Sheffield number.

The Ivory Clock, *page 45*

It was during the sixth conducted tour that the ivory clock was stolen. It was then that Ferdinand Muscatel's attention was diverted by his friend the bus driver. The thief must have belonged to a group which actually included a visit to the Green Drawing Room. But if it had been one of the earlier tours, Ferdie would have been bound to notice that the clock was missing.

The Telephone Hoax, *page 50*

Arne Larsen may have had a fabulous memory, but he couldn't count! The long description as well as the illustration show clearly that it was not a gang of seven, but a gang of six.

The Tell-Tale Diary, *page 56*

The first thing to arouse the inspector's suspicion was the fact that the diary started on December 31. Now there isn't a law saying you mustn't begin a diary on that or any other day, but most people would have waited until New Year's day, January 1. So it didn't sound genuine from the word go.

Caroline's important mistake, however, was to pay no attention to the days of the week. If

December 31 was a Wednesday, then it was unlikely she would have bought a zipper for her yellow blouse on January 4, for that was a Sunday, a day when department stores are usually closed. As a result, Inspector Kramer was convinced that the "diary" had been hastily made up by Caroline in an attempt to throw dust in the eyes of the police, in case they succeeded in tracking her down.

Blackmail with Music, page 64

Max Major was the culprit. Although Bernard Martin said only that Frank Bull had been seen "borrowing a piece of the firm's equipment," Major knew without being told that it was an electronic calculator. Besides, he was the only one with an obvious accomplice, his nephew Ben. Ben had been told what to say over the phone to Mr. Bull, who would otherwise have been likely to recognize Major's voice.

Mrs. Angel—Witness, page 78

These are the three contradictions in Mrs. Angel's statements:
1. On the phone, she spoke of a delivery van. Later, the van had changed to a car. And if

the men put the furs in the trunk, it must certainly have been a car, rather than a van.

2. In her first version, the vehicle was pulling up outside the fur shop when she caught sight of it. Her second account declared that the car was already parked there.

3. Mrs. Angel's first description stated that the thieves cut a hole in the display window. Her later statement talked about the men smashing the window, presumably with a brick.

The Blackout, page 83

The police could easily provide evidence that "The Stowaway" hadn't been screened that evening as scheduled, but that a live show jumping program had been substituted at the last minute.

The Terrible Twins, page 87

Both boys must have been involved in the lighter's disappearance. According to Uncle Nick, his nephews should not have known of its existence. But Peter let the cat out of the bag by showing that he knew it was in the closet; and Paul would not have referred to his uncle's bedroom unless he had been poking about there.

Rent-A-Ghost, page 92

If Oliver hadn't left the reception area all evening, how did he know that it was Mrs. Woodmaker who had been robbed? Sir John said simply that "a thief . . . had struck."

Geraniums for Polly, page 98

The fifth floor tenant was to blame.

We can safely assume that if the damage to Polly's roof was so great, the pot was thrown from a considerable height. This excludes both the ground floor and the third floor residents. We can also assume that the culprit did not wish to be seen, and in that case, the mischief was done from the only upper window from which no light was showing, the one on the fifth floor.

Paul Crabbe is Missing, page 102

1. Perry Clifton asked Dr. Donald Dorset, "Can't you at least tell us where Crabbe is now?" To which Dr. Dorset replied, "I'm sorry, I've no idea. . . ." So it was clear that he knew perfectly well that his patient was actually Paul Crabbe, and that Chivers was a false name.

2. Lionel Winston had told Jamie Stokes that he was going straight home after seeing him that morning. So if Stokes had had a message for Winston, he would have sent someone to his house. If in fact that person came to see him at Enrico's, he ought to have guessed that he had been followed.